MURDER ON THE TOR

AN EXHAM-ON-SEA MYSTERY

FRANCES EVESHAM

Boldwood

First published in Great Britain in 2020 by Boldwood Books Ltd.

Copyright © Frances Evesham, 2020

Cover Design by Nick Castle Design

A CIP catalogue record for this book is available from the British Library.

Paperback ISBN 978-1-80048-019-3

Large Print ISBN 978-1-80048-020-9

Ebook ISBN 978-1-80048-022-3

Kindle ISBN 978-1-80048-021-6

Boldwood Books Ltd
23 Bowerdean Street
London SW6 3TN
www.boldwoodbooks.com

1

GLASTONBURY TOR

Sunlight bathed the ruined tower in gold. Libby leaned on a stile at the base of Glastonbury Tor, looking up at the summit far above, Bear by her side. The huge sheepdog panted, tongue lolling, keen to begin their favourite climb. 'Wait, Bear.' Libby's fingers sank into coarse, thick fur round the dog's neck as, mesmerised, she watched the first pearly wisps of mist rise, shift and coalesce. Soon, a heavy grey blanket cloaked the hill, blotting out the tower on the summit and the sun's rays.

She loved to walk on the Tor in the early morning. Her first visit had been years ago, when she'd spent a holiday in Exham on Sea with Trevor, her late husband, and the children. The whole family had loved the windy climb to the top to see Somerset spread below.

Those had been happy days, before Trevor became so difficult and controlling.

Bear barked, shattering the silence. He slid from under Libby's hand and bounded up the slope, mouth wide, paws muffled on the grass. Libby ran, breath rasping, legs trembling with effort. 'Come back,' she called, but the dog disappeared into the mist without a backward glance. Libby ran a few more steps and stopped to breathe, suddenly reluctant to follow.

What was that? A single howl drifted out from the cloud. Libby took a step into the damp mass and the mist closed in, chilling her lungs. Strands of wet hair clung to her cheeks, but she brushed them aside and climbed higher, isolated and blind, sliding on the grass. Her feet stumbled on to a solid path and she followed the easier track, expecting every moment to break through the mist. Time and distance shifted, until she had no idea how long she'd been walking.

Just as she began to think she'd be stuck in the white wilderness all day, she burst through a swirl of damp cotton wool cloud into a blaze of light. She blinked, blinded by the sudden glare, and the tense knot in her stomach unwound. Glorious sunshine bathed the top of the Tor, warm on her face. In the brilliant morning light, St Michael's Tower stood out, sharp against a blue sky. In a burst of relief, energised, legs no longer tired, Libby followed a series of steps cut into the hill, climbing fast. 'Bear? Where are you?' Her voice carried, thin and high in the morning air, but the dog was out of sight.

Libby sank onto a wooden bench, watching the mist below. A sound at her back brought her to her feet, nerves jangling. A small girl, hair a tangled mass of black curls, stared, motionless, eyes wide, clutching a furry brown toy monkey. Libby smiled. 'Hello. You made me jump.' The child snuggled a cheek into the monkey's fur. Libby tried again. 'Is Mummy here?' The girl shook her head. 'Daddy?' The round eyes slid away from Libby's face. 'You're not alone, are you?' The child stuck a thumb in her mouth and sucked.

Libby remembered Bear. 'Did you see my dog? A big, cuddly one. He's up here, somewhere.' The girl smiled, showing tiny white teeth, and pointed up the hill to the tower. Libby screwed up her eyes against the sun but saw no sign of Bear. A finger of ice crept up her back. She shivered and turned to speak to the child but the words froze on her tongue. The girl had disappeared.

'This is ridiculous.' Libby spoke out loud. She was letting the Tor get on her nerves. The child must have wandered down through the mist to a waiting parent. She wouldn't come to much harm on the Tor.

Libby marched on up the hill, as fast as her wobbly legs allowed, determined to shake off her unease. She'd been reading too many stories of Glastonbury and King Arthur's ghost.

She turned the final corner of the zig-zag path in record time, with no further stops. Such a feat would normally fill her with pride, but today, Libby was too worried about Bear. She covered the remaining few yards at a run and stepped into the cool, dark, deserted interior of St Michael's Tower.

Crossing the flagstones in three quick strides, she was back in daylight. Bear lay on the grass, ears flat, tail twitching. 'There you are.' The dog's tail flickered as he staggered to his feet. 'What's wrong?' His head hung low, the fur of his neck standing out in a prickly ruff.

Libby knelt by Bear's side and slipped her arms round his chest. 'Are you hurt?' She ran gentle fingers over the animal's body, searching for lumps and bumps, finding none. She lifted the coarse top layer of hair and inspected the soft inner coat for blood, but there was no injury to be seen. She scrambled to her feet and, hands on hips, gazed over the mist that hid the nearby fields and woods to a range of distant hills, shimmering blue in the sunshine.

A stiff breeze sent her to seek shelter on the other side of the Tower, where she sank on to the grass, back propped against the ancient stones, and drew both knees up to her chest. Her gaze swept in an arc, searching for signs of company. No one appeared but at least she had Bear as a companion. Libby pulled the huge animal close, glad of his earthy, doggy smell. 'What happened, Bear? What frightened you?' She rubbed the dog's head. 'This place gives me the creeps.'

Her right leg hurt. She shifted position, rubbing her calf, and searched in the grass, curious, expecting to find an abandoned shard of glass or the ring from a beer can. Instead, her fingers closed on one smooth, round pebble, then another. She searched until she'd uncovered a handful of muddy beads joined by a length of rusty wire.

Libby rubbed the stones and the mud fell away to reveal a necklace of even, smooth beads that glowed golden-red, as radiant as the sunshine. *Amber.* Libby dropped them into her pocket and called to the dog. 'Come on, Bear. Time to go.'

* * *

Listless, the dog plodded down the hill, staying close to Libby's side, tail tucked under his body. The mist still blocked their path and Libby hesitated, reluctant to step back into the clammy white blanket. Bear whined. 'You don't like it either, do you? I wish we could find another way down.' Unless they intended to stay on the Tor until every last trace of murk had dispersed, she'd have to face it. 'Take a deep breath, Bear, and follow me.'

She pulled her jacket tight. 'Right, here we go.' This time, she took only half a dozen steps before bursting out into the June sunshine, laughing, relieved beyond common sense. She reached over to pat the dog. 'That wasn't so scary, was it?'

Bear whined, shivering despite the warmth of the sun. He coughed. 'You can't have caught a cold, not in just half an hour.' The dog coughed once more and slowed his pace, struggling to keep up with Libby. Every few paces, he stopped to sniff the ground. 'Did you see something that frightened you?' Libby asked. 'I can't take you back in this state. What will Max say? I only borrowed you because I wanted to stretch my legs and everyone else was busy.'

When she'd called to collect the dog for their walk, early that morning, Libby found Max Ramshore engaged in an animated phone conversation. He opened the door, grinned, winked and gave a thumbs-up sign. By the time Libby finished snapping Bear's lead to his collar, Max was scribbling notes on a pad of paper. He'd taken early retirement from his banking career and now undertook various consultancies. Libby had only a vague idea what this meant. Max had a habit of avoiding her questions, admitting only to tracking shady financial deals. He was too engrossed in the call to stop and talk, so Libby waved and led Bear to her small, battered but much loved purple Citroen.

The noise of a car, brakes squealing as it screeched to a halt, brought Libby back to the present. Doors slammed. Raised voices floated up the hill and, in a flurry of movement and shouting, two figures burst from the woods. The uniformed police officer in the lead ignored Libby and staggered on up the Hill. A policeman in plain clothes followed and Libby groaned. Blond, blue eyed, the man was easily recognisable as Max's son.

Detective Sergeant Joe Ramshore stopped in front of Libby; weary exasperation written on his face. 'I don't believe it, Mrs Forest. Always in on the action, aren't you?' He waved to his companion, urging him to keep running. Libby recognised Constable Evans, older, stouter and less fit than Joe, round face brick-red with effort, panting and gasping as he stumbled higher.

Joe groaned. 'I might have known you'd be involved, Mrs Forest. Did you phone it in?' His raised eyebrows and folded arms made Libby feel like a criminal. It must be a trick he learned at police college. Her fingers closed on the beads, safe in her pocket. Did he intend to accuse her of theft?

More police appeared; too many, surely, to search for a single string of amber beads. Close to the summit, a fitter, younger officer overtook Evans. A dreadful thought struck Libby, turning her hands clammy. 'Has something happened to the little girl?'

'Girl? What girl? We had a call about a dead man on the Tor. Was it you on the phone? Did you see him?'

Libby pulled out her phone, waving it at the detective. 'I haven't made any calls today.'

Joe narrowed his eyes, reluctant to believe anything without proof. 'Well, someone did. You need to go, Mrs Forest. We're about to cordon off the Tor.'

'There was a child on the hill, but she disappeared.' The mist seemed to thicken again. Or was it Libby's eyes, as they strained to focus against the sun? She took a step towards the Tower.

Joe swung round. 'Keep away, now. This is a police matter.'

2

SWEET TEA

Libby dragged a listless Bear back to the car, fear lying heavy in her chest. A death on the hill. *Not the child, please. Not that little girl.* Libby's lips shaped the words, repeating them under her breath as though they were a mantra.

Joe said it was a man. A dead man. Libby clung to the thought, but her heart still thudded and bile rose in her throat. If something dreadful happened to the curly haired girl, it would be Libby's fault; her responsibility. She should have grabbed one of the small hands, chaperoned the child into town and refused to rest until she found the parents.

Channels on the car radio buzzed and blared as Libby drove back to Exham. The local station was playing a jaunty tune that ended abruptly, cut off. A presenter's broad Bristolian vowels made the announcement, his words drawn out, savouring the drama. 'A body has been discovered on Glastonbury Tor. Police have yet to make a statement. The body's believed to be that of an elderly man, but we have no confirmation as yet. Our reporter is at the scene and we'll bring you breaking news as it happens...' Libby's hands gripped the steering wheel until they hurt. A rush of relief brought hot tears to her eyes, scorching the eyelids. An old man had died but at least the little girl was safe.

Bear whined, dragging Libby back to the present. She forced a shaky hand from the wheel and fumbled the key out of the ignition. Her thoughts raced. How did the body come to be on the Tor? 'Did you see anything strange, Bear? Something I missed?' She glanced over one shoulder. The dog whined again, and Libby touched his nose. It felt hot and dry. 'Poor old fellow, you don't seem at all well.'

She snatched a glance at her phone. Ten thirty? That couldn't be right. Had the battery given out or something? She switched off the phone and waited, counting to five before hitting the restart button, but there was no mistake. Most of the morning had slipped away despite their expedition starting so early. Libby calculated. A six thirty arrival and the climb to the summit; a brief conversation with the child; a rest at the top while she found the necklace. How could that have lasted four hours?

She must have wandered in the mist, following a circular path, disorientated, for longer than she realised. No wonder her legs ached. She shivered, one hand resting on Bear's head. She'd never seen the dog so exhausted. Bred to walk for hours in the mountains of Romania, he was usually a ball of boundless energy. 'I can't take you back to Max in this state.' There was a veterinary practice on the road leading to the beach. Before Libby took Bear home, she'd get him checked over. She'd never forgive herself if anything happened to the animal.

* * *

Bear hung back at the door of the surgery, reluctant, eyes mournful. 'I can't carry you. You're far too heavy. It's no good looking so miserable.' It took Libby a combination of pushing, pulling and pleading to coax him through the door.

'Poor thing,' murmured the receptionist, a cheerful, middle-aged woman. 'Isn't that the dog old Mr Thomson used to own? I'm sure Tanya will fit him in straight away. It's a quiet day, today.' She muttered into a telephone. After a moment the vet appeared, pulling on a pair of blue disposable gloves and beckoning Libby and Bear into a consulting room.

Tanya Ross, the vet, had a wiry, lean body that hinted at a jogging habit, despite the woman's apparent age. *Older than me. In much better shape, too.* Libby pulled in her stomach. Only five foot, four inches, tall, she knew every ounce of spare flesh on her body showed. The vet must be well over retirement age, judging by the ruddy, outdoor complexion and collection of crows' feet round her eyes, but she skipped across the floor, quick and light, eyes robin-bright, to examine the dog with firm but gentle fingers. Bear lifted his head and licked her hand.

Libby's spirits rose. 'He's feeling better, already. Must be your magic touch.' By the time the vet finished weighing, measuring and inspecting the dog, Bear looked far more cheerful; almost back to normal. 'What do you think was the matter?'

Tanya Ross fondled Bear's ears. 'His temperature's low but he seems to be recovering fast. What happened? Has he had a shock, or been chilled?'

Libby swallowed. 'It sounds stupid, but when the mist came down on the Tor, we lost our way. We were on the hill far longer than I thought, in the damp and cold. I can't understand how it happened. We must have been there for an hour or more, wandering round the sides of the Tor. It gave me the creeps, to be honest, and we'd only just got out of the mist when the police arrived. They told me about an accident on the hill; about the man who died.'

Tanya Ross put her head on one side. 'I heard it on the news. If you were on the hill when that poor man died, it must have given you a nasty shock. I think you need a nice hot cup of tea. Have a seat in the waiting room, and I'll make one. I could do with a brew.'

She disappeared through another door while Libby and Bear returned to the waiting room, which smelled of dog and disinfectant. Libby passed the time looking at cute photos of kittens and puppies, reading a poster that warned of the danger of ticks, and admiring a row of framed certificates. She examined all four, one for each of the vets in the practice. She'd guessed Tanya Ross's age accurately. The oldest of the team, she'd graduated from Bristol University way back in 1971 The newest vet, younger than Libby's son, Robert, had been in practice for no more than two years.

There was nothing else to read and Libby settled on a hard, wooden chair. At once, the receptionist stopped pretending to work at a computer and took off her glasses, bursting with news. Her eyes sparkled. 'Have you heard about the dead man?'

'I just came from Glastonbury Tor,' Libby admitted.

She soon wished she'd held her tongue for the woman licked her lips and, face alight with excitement, whispered, 'Did you see the body?'

'No. It was misty on the hill.' Libby kept her answer brief, hoping to shut down the conversation, but she was disappointed. The receptionist, thrilled, drew a long breath through pursed lips. 'Ooh, you be careful, m'dear. You don't want to be going up the Tor, not in the mist. Anyone will tell you that.'

Libby raised an eyebrow, suddenly intrigued. 'Why not?'

The receptionist leaned over the counter. 'You're new around here – I forgot. You see, some say there are tunnels under the Tor and King Arthur walks there every midsummer, guarded by the little people. Folk around here don't go up on the hill, then. They reckon if one of the fairies appears, it heralds a death.' Before Libby, stunned, could reply, the vet reappeared. The receptionist snatched up her spectacles, replaced them on her nose and resumed typing.

'Here.' Tanya Ross offered Libby a battered mug. 'Strong, with milk and two sugars.' Libby took a polite sip, trying not to wrinkle her nose. She hated sugar in tea. The vet leaned an elbow on the counter. 'I bet Mrs White's been telling you tales about strange happenings on the Tor.' The receptionist typed harder; eyes fixed on the screen. 'Oh, yes,' the vet went on. 'Everyone round here will tell you that local people keep away when the mist comes down.' She raised her voice. 'Don't they, Mrs White?'

The receptionist pretended not to hear. Tanya rolled her eyes. 'Take no notice of her, Mrs Forest. The stories are meant to excite the tourists, though I bet there weren't many other walkers up there today.'

'No. Oddly enough, there weren't. Bear and I were alone at first. Then we met a little girl. And the dead man—'

'You saw him?'

Libby drained the mug, trying not to shudder. 'No. He wasn't on the hill when we arrived, and I can't understand how he managed to reach the top unseen.'

'Ah. He must have climbed up the other path.'

Libby started. 'There's another one?'

'Oh yes. There's the easy way, through the woods...'

'That's the route I took.'

'And there's another entrance further down the road. The second path is shorter, but steeper.'

Libby's laugh was shaky. 'So, I'm not crazy. He came from the other direction. I didn't see him because I was lost in the mist.'

'Any idea how he died?'

'The police didn't say.'

'A heart attack, that's most likely. It's a steepish climb if you're not used to exercise.'

An elderly lady burst through the surgery door, struggling to control two perfectly matched Scottie dogs, as neat as a pair of white porcelain figurines. Tanya Ross handed Libby a small box. 'Put a couple of these tablets in Bear's food. They'll keep him calm for the next few hours and he'll be right as rain soon.'

She presented a hefty bill. Libby blinked, recovered, paid and left, the dog trotting at her side, tail in the air as though nothing had ever been wrong.

'You're a fraud,' Libby hissed, 'and an expensive one, at that.'

3

MAX

'Imagine, Max, while Bear and I were on the Tor, someone died.'
Max's open French doors led to a vast, well maintained garden.
Bear, his usual rude health restored, chased imaginary rabbits
under bushes. He nudged aside a voluptuous peony's blowsy pink
and white flowers and scrabbled at the earth beneath, sending up
a shower of soil. Triumphant, he galloped back to drop a filthy,
bedraggled tennis ball at Libby's feet. 'The mist, and Bear vanish-
ing, and seeing that strange little girl.' Libby shivered. 'No wonder
Bear had a funny turn.'

Max scoffed. 'He tired himself and got cold. Nothing strange
about it. It sounds as though you wandered around, confused, for
a lot longer than you realised.'

'I think I panicked a bit,' Libby admitted. 'I lost my bearings. I
thought I was on a path.'

'You were. It's the ancient way up the hill. The remains of
seven terraces still spiral round the Tor, like a maze. They're
visible from a helicopter, but hard to see when you're walking.
Legend suggests the monks from the Abbey took that path, when
they processed up the hill to the Tower. It takes a while to reach

the top, because it's an indirect route, but it's easier than climbing straight up. The steps you used at the top are recent additions, intended to make it easier for visitors. You walked the ancient route.'

Libby grunted. 'I didn't enjoy it, and nor did Bear.'

Max looked serious. 'Don't forget, Bear's an old fellow and he won't be with us for ever. In dog years, he must be getting on for ninety. I'll miss the old chap as much as you when he goes, but I'm not surprised he feels under the weather from time to time.'

'At least he recovered quickly. I didn't want to bring him back in that state.' Libby wiped mud from the ball. 'Tanya Ross's receptionist would like me to believe some kind of curse jinxed poor Bear. Something to do with Glastonbury's special relationship with the spirit world.'

'Don't let local people hear you scoff, because we're fond of our Glastonbury legends around here. We all know King Arthur's buried under the Tor.'

Libby threw Bear's ball at Max. Damp and grubby, it left a smudge of mud on his shoulder. 'Oops. Sorry.' She scrubbed at Max's jacket with a tissue, making matters worse. 'The Once and Future King is also rumoured to be buried in about five other places in England, according to the stories.'

She gave up on the mud stain. 'Joking apart, it was strange and scary on the hill today. In that thick mist, I lost all sense of time and place. I could have walked in circles for hours. It made me shiver, and I'm not given to imagining things.'

Max tossed the ball to Bear, who loped down the garden in pursuit. 'There's no one more down to earth than you.'

'Thank you.' She guessed that was meant to be some sort of compliment, though it made Libby sound dull. 'Anyway, after we came out of the mist, Joe arrived. The police spread out all over the hill, looking for the body. It gave me a shock, so soon after meeting that funny little girl.'

Max closed the doors and rested a pair of size twelve feet on the coffee table. 'I bet that child ran straight down to the nearest play park. Kids scuttle up and down the Tor all the time. The parents are always near – just don't have the puff to keep up.'

His easy explanation infuriated Libby. He wasn't taking her seriously. 'Max, someone died up there. I can't just ignore it.'

'You could leave it to the police.'

Libby made a face. 'They're most likely to write it off as an accident.'

Max sighed. 'It's none of our business.'

Libby took a breath, and Max raised his hands, as if warding off a blow. 'Don't shout at me. The police are perfectly capable of investigating a sudden death, especially if the man died from a heart attack. But the history of the Tor's interesting. I've got a book, somewhere...' He covered the floor in two strides and ran his hand over a long shelf.

Dozens of volumes, crammed in at all angles, jostled for every inch of space. 'No, must have left it in the study. Come with me.' Curious, Libby followed Max out of the room. He grinned over one shoulder. 'Don't often take people into my study. Ignore the mess if you can.'

On three sides of the tiny room, shelves ran from floor to ceiling. A haphazard mix of ancient, saggy, mismatched chairs hinted at long, comfortable reading sessions. An oak desk occupied most of the floor space. Intrigued, Libby tilted her head to one side, trying to read the spines on a heap of books that teetered on a nearby stool. *International Corporate Finance.* Max straightened the pile. 'Work, I'm afraid.'

'Sorry. Didn't mean to pry. It's one of my bad habits. My children tell me I'm nosy.'

'Nonsense. Curiosity's a great quality. What with that and your brain power, it's no wonder you can't resist problem solving. Especially when you think other people aren't taking the issue seriously.' Max shot her a grin as he brushed crumbs and dog hairs from a chair. 'Would you like the guided tour?'

'No, the Glastonbury book first, if you don't mind.'

'Well, come and look round another time. This is a favourite place of mine.' Max waved an arm round the room. 'See, there's your cookbook.' Libby fingered *More Baking at the Beach,* a second collection of her favourite cake recipes. She had to admit, Christian, her publisher, had made a good job of the book in the end. She'd forgive him for the ceaseless phone calls and emails asking her to explain her recipes. Max was kind to buy a copy; she couldn't imagine him ever making use of it.

Max's finger traced the volumes on the shelves, stopping at a green, leather covered tome. 'Here. *Myths and Legends of the West Country.* You can borrow it, if you want.'

'Thanks.' She took the book, smooth and cool under her fingers. 'I love this room. It's cosy.' Every object looked right, from the rows of books, to the massive dog basket in one corner.

'Me too. I rattle around in the rest of this place. Can't imagine why I bought such a big house.' He waved at the ceiling. 'An old rectory like this should be full of life, with dozens of kids running up the stairs, kicking the walls and fighting. A grumpy old retired banker has no right to live here alone.'

Satisfied the chair was sufficiently clean, Max plumped up the cushions and waved Libby to sit. 'Read *Myths and Legends* and you'll understand how lucky you've been to escape the grip of the Tor. Why, you could have been whisked away to Fairyland.' Max grinned. His old fisherman's sweater was unravelling round the neck, giving him the appearance of a North Sea trawler captain. Libby caught a whiff of woody aftershave.

'Incidentally,' Max fiddled with documents on the desk, not meeting Libby's eye. 'I'm going to a photography exhibition tomorrow. I wondered if you'd be interested.' He dropped the papers in a drawer and paced round the room.

A smile tugged at the corners of Libby's mouth. 'What photos?' She giggled as a blush crept over Max's face. 'Yours? Don't tell me you're an ace photographer?'

He stopped walking and settled into a battered old chair; long legs stretched across the floor. 'Nothing so grand, I'm afraid, but you can't live in the West Country and not be tempted to take a snap or two. I've submitted a few pictures to the show. Most of the exhibitors are keen amateurs, but a local man, John Williams, is a professional, selling pictures to magazines like Country Life. He's showing some of his earliest work. A retrospective, I believe, is the proper term.'

Libby was more interested in the sudden glimpse into one of Max's passions. 'Can I see your photos?'

'Not now. I'd be embarrassed. Come to the show, tomorrow. The hall's in Glastonbury, funnily enough, and the exhibition's the brainchild of Chesterton Wendlebury and the company he works for, Pritchards. It's called Somerset Secrets. The idea is to show off the county for the summer visitors.'

Libby groaned. She'd met Wendlebury, a wealthy businessman with a finger stuck firmly in most local pies, many times. He sat on the boards of several big, ruthless and avaricious companies. She'd suspected Pritchards, Wendlebury's biggest business, of planning to take over the Exham bakery, putting Libby, her lodger, Mandy, and Frank Brown, the baker, out of business.

Libby disliked Mr Wendlebury more every time they met.

* * *

The doorbell interrupted. 'I thought I'd find you here.' Max waved his son, Detective Sergeant Joe, into the hall. The policeman stepped inside, awkward, as though he hadn't been near his father's home for a while. 'Haven't got much time,' he said. 'Can't stop long. Wanted to let you know about the body on Glastonbury Tor.'

Joe was a younger edition of his father. He'd inherited the enigmatic, crooked smile and a pair of ice-blue eyes, the legacy of a Norwegian ancestry. At least the two of them were talking these days. By all accounts, they'd spent most of Joe's adult life at daggers drawn, since Max's divorce from Joe's mother.

'I heard the brief details on the radio,' Libby said. 'But they didn't say much. Just that it was an elderly man. What happened? Who was he?'

'The name's John Williams. He had a wallet in his pocket with his address. He lives – lived alone.'

Max paused in the act of opening a bag of coffee. 'John Williams? The photographer?'

'Is he?'

'Half the exhibition tomorrow is his work.' Max was thoughtful. 'I wonder if it'll go ahead?'

Libby interrupted. 'How did he die, Joe?'

Joe thrust his hands in his pockets. 'Suicide.'

Libby snorted.

'I know what you're thinking, Mrs Forest. You'd prefer it to be murder, but he had a note in his pocket.'

'You think he killed himself? The day before his exhibition?' Libby didn't even try to hide her disbelief.

The police officer wagged a finger, infuriating Libby. 'Mrs Forest, everything points to suicide.'

'You've said that before.' Libby had twice proved murder when the police had dismissed a death, calling it an accident.

'It's an open and shut case.'

Libby folded her arms. 'It's too easy to write off every death as accident or suicide.'

Max intervened, grinning, clearly enjoying the argument. 'You can't blame the police. Funding, lack of time, shortage of manpower...'

'What about justice? Doesn't every sudden death deserve investigation?'

Joe groaned. 'In a perfect world,' he said, 'of course they do. The world isn't perfect, though. We can't waste hundreds of police hours trying to prove a man was murdered when he left a perfectly clear note.'

He shrugged. 'And before you ask, it's in his own handwriting. We checked it with shopping lists and so on. And he tied a plastic bag round his head. Easy to do it yourself if you're determined enough – not that I'm offering tips. No one else need be involved. So, unless someone provides evidence to the contrary, suicide it is. My constable's doing the paperwork, right now.'

Max laid a restraining hand on Libby's arm. 'And you came to tell us because...?'

Joe coloured. 'Ah. Thought you'd be interested.'

Max said, 'You mean, you've got a few doubts of your own and you wouldn't mind if we poked around?'

Joe's face was impassive. 'I couldn't possibly ask it of a pair of civilians.'

'Of course, you can't. And you haven't, have you?' Max winked.

'Will the exhibition go ahead tomorrow?' Libby asked.

Max grunted. 'If I know Chesterton Wendlebury, he won't let a little thing like a tragedy get in the way of a money making venture. He'll be hoping John Williams' death makes the show more profitable.'

Joe rubbed his chin. 'Maybe I'll send someone along to keep an eye on things. We can spare a community support officer for an hour or two.'

Libby asked, 'Did you find the girl I saw?'

'We spoke to a couple of local people.' Joe gave a short laugh. 'Amazing how news can spread. There were crowds in Glastonbury by the time the body was removed. At least it saved us some legwork.'

'The child...' she prompted.

'Well, we heard the usual tales about fairies whose appearance heralds untimely death, of course, but aside from those, there are no reports of any missing children. I don't think you need worry.'

His radio buzzed. He flicked a switch and listened. 'I've got to get back to the station. Keep your ears to the ground, will you?'

4

MANDY

As she tidied the kitchen after breakfast the next day, Libby related her adventures on the Tor to her lodger and fellow baker's assistant, Mandy. Exham's resident teenage Goth flicked her head. A lock of black hair fell back over one side of her face. Libby closed one eye, trying to decide which side of Mandy's head looked oddest; the left, shaved close to the skull, or the right with its single long, limp strand reaching to the girl's chin. Libby longed to push in a hair clip.

Mandy jigged from one foot to the other. 'Are you going to investigate the dead man? Can I help?'

'There's little to go on at the moment. We're off to the photographic exhibition today, to see some of his work.'

'We? Max is going, too?' Mandy examined her fingernails, selected one and nibbled the corner. 'So, you're going on a date with him.'

'It's not a date, it's an investigation. You can come, too, if you like.'

'Not likely. I'm off to one of Steve's rehearsals after work.'

'Band or orchestra?'

'Band. His mate lent him a new mouthpiece for the saxophone.' Steve, Mandy's boyfriend, was a talented musician headed for the Royal College of Music in September. Meanwhile, he divided his skills. Sometimes, neatly suited, he played classical clarinet in an orchestra with other soon-to-be professional musicians. On other days, in black t-shirt and nose rings, he contributed the saxophone part to a local band called Effluvium.

'Why does he need a new mouthpiece?'

'It's metal. Makes more noise.' Libby winced and Mandy giggled. 'Yeah. It's loud. His mum won't let him play it in the house. Anyway, Mrs F, don't change the subject. You've got a date.'

'It's not a date.'

Mandy giggled. 'Saying it don't make it true. Bet you a tenner he comes in the Jag. You can't go on a proper date in that old Land Rover.' It was true, Max's favourite vehicle did smell a little of dog and ancient leather.

'Ten pounds? It's a deal.'

'Don't forget your meeting with Jumbles, that posh shop in Bath, this afternoon.'

'I'll be there,' Libby promised. 'I'll have plenty of time. I'll nip back here, pick up the samples and get to the meeting with time to spare.'

Last night, Libby's experiment with new chocolate flavours had extended well into the early hours of the morning. Samples of new orange and geranium creams sat in neat boxes in the shiny, professional standard kitchen, along with Exham's favourites, lemon meringue and mint. Libby had prepared everything for today's meeting. She wasn't leaving matters to chance. If Jumbles put in a big order, *Mrs Forest's Chocolates* would be on the way to making a decent profit.

Mandy, selecting a new finger to bite, raised heavy black eyebrows. 'Whatever.'

Libby chewed her lower lip. Mandy was turning into a real asset in the fast growing chocolate business, despite her weird appearance. Could Libby afford to take her on full time? Frank's bakery, the main outlet, was doing well. The business had gone from strength to strength lately. Frank, the owner, was so delighted he'd offered Libby a partnership. That would mean changes.

Libby wouldn't have time to manage all the development, manufacture and packaging herself much longer, never mind the marketing and advertising, especially if outlets like Jumbles put in regular orders. She'd been thinking of setting up a proper apprenticeship. She'd talk to Frank, sure he'd agree.

Would Mandy commit to it? 'We need a proper business meeting soon. I'd like to run a few ideas past you.'

'So long as you provide cake for the meeting, Mrs F. Oh, there's the door. I'll get it.'

'No...' Too late.

Mandy raced down the hall and threw open the door. 'Mr Ramshore. You look wicked.' She edged round the new arrival to take a peek at his car. 'You've brought your new Jag. How very – er – appropriate.'

Max looked puzzled. 'Swallowed a dictionary, have you, Mandy?'

The girl held out a hand, palm up, to Libby, who sighed and scrabbled in the handbag hooked on to the banister. 'Little bet, that's all,' Libby muttered, and pressed a folded ten pound note into Mandy's outstretched hand.

* * *

'These are terrific. I'd no idea there were so many fantastic beauty spots near Exham.' Libby and Max sauntered down the rows of photographs. 'I love that sunset on Exham beach. The one with the lighthouse in the distance.'

He didn't answer. 'Max, are you listening?' She'd never seen him so embarrassed. 'It's one of yours, isn't it? I'm going to buy it.'

'I'll give you a copy if you really want it.'

'No, you bought my book, so I'll buy your photograph. Oh, here's Chesterton.' Chesterton Wendlebury, burly with a yellow waistcoat, a thatch of grey hair and an impressive Roman nose, appeared beside Max. Libby's friend, Marina, splendid in a floor length orange and green dress, a red and yellow pashmina, and a string of purple beads, followed hard on his heels accompanied by a small, balding, elderly man in a formal suit. If ever there was an odd couple, it was Marina and Henry, her mild mannered husband.

Libby more often met Marina accompanied by the powerful, larger-than-life Chesterton Wendlebury than by Henry. She suspected they were more than friends.

'Henry.' Marina possessed an ear shattering, retired deputy head teacher voice. 'You simply have to buy this one. It's utterly perfect for your study.'

'Sorry, Marina,' Libby intervened. 'It's taken. I'm afraid I got here first.'

Marina looked down her substantial nose. 'I don't see any little red dot.'

'I haven't had a chance to finalise the deal.' Libby stood her ground.

'Well, you're too late, because I'm determined to have it. Chester, here's my card. Put a red dot on the picture, right now. Libby won't mind, will you, dear?'

Marina, as ever, expected her own way but Libby wouldn't give up without a fight. She wanted Max's photograph. 'In fact, I do mind, Marina. I saw it first.' They stood toe to toe, hands on hips, like children in a school playground.

Libby pasted a wide smile on her face. 'I was wondering if you still wanted me to take Shipley out for a walk tomorrow?' Marina would rather die than take her own dog for a walk. 'You know, I'm so busy these days, it's getting hard to find the time...'

Marina took the hint. 'Of course, you must have the picture, darling.' She waved an arm that jangled with bracelets, making a quick recovery. 'I wouldn't dream of standing in your way if it means so much to you.' She peered at the printed label below the photograph. 'M.R. That wouldn't be you, Max, by any chance?' She laughed, reminding Libby of the donkey whose loud braying call sounded across the fields in the early summer mornings. 'Maybe Henry and I will choose another of your efforts, Max. I'm sure we can find a nice one somewhere. Won't we, Henry?'

'Yes, dear. Perhaps we will.' Marina departed like a frigate in full sail as Chesterton Wendlebury stuck the all-important red dot to the photograph.

Max took Libby's arm. 'I think a cup of tea might be a good idea before you start a fight.'

He steered Libby to the single unoccupied table in the refreshment corner. The hall had filled almost to capacity, now the news of John Williams' death was out. Who could resist an exhibition of photographs by a man who'd died only the day before? The place hummed with excitement. Near the entrance, high visibility jackets marked the presence of a pair of police community support officers. It was their frustrating task to field a constant stream of theories, for everyone had an opinion on the affair, no matter how little they knew the dead photographer.

Chesterton Wendlebury stalked the rows of easels, hands behind his back, every smug inch the man in charge of a successful event. The till clanged and dinged. At this rate, all the exhibits would be sold in less than an hour.

Libby took a sip of weak, lukewarm coffee, made a wry face and replaced the sturdy green cup in its saucer. *I think I'll wait.*

'That's Catriona.' The muttered exclamation caught Libby's attention. At the end of a row of prints on stands, a short woman, so squat as to be almost square, had pressed a hand to her mouth, stifling her exclamation. The woman sent a quick, furtive glance around the room, as though checking for observers, before grabbing the photo and sliding it inside her coat.

She hurried down the row, removing one photo after another from its display easel.

She was stealing.

Libby shouted. 'Hey! What are you doing? Are those your photos?'

The woman, caught off balance, stumbled. Her foot nudged one leg of the nearest picture stand. It wobbled. She turned away, walking fast, head held high. Eyes fixed on the door, looking neither to right nor left, she cannoned into Libby's table sending coffee splashing across the surface.

Libby, transfixed, ignored the coffee as the picture stand rocked, teetered, righted itself for a split second and at last, in slow motion, toppled over.

It crashed onto the next stand.

The second easel fell against a third and momentum built down the row.

One after another, each easel thundering into the next, they fell like a set of dominoes. The last stand in the row collapsed on the floor in a muddle of wooden legs and photographic prints.

The woman who'd taken the photographs dodged a knot of stunned spectators as she made a dash for the door. She would have got clear away but for Chesterton Wendlebury, who stepped out, his bulk filling the exit doors, to stop the woman in her tracks. 'Not so fast, madam.'

5

JEMIMA

The culprit's eyes, enormous behind the lenses of a pair of glasses rimmed with tortoiseshell, filled with tears. 'Oh dear,' she murmured. 'Dear me. I didn't mean to...'

She sniffed, fumbled in her bag, pulled out a handkerchief and blew her nose. 'It was an accident. I – I tripped over an easel, and then – then they all started to fall, and I – well, I suppose I panicked.' She shot a sly glance at Wendlebury, as if assessing the effect of her words.

Wendlebury was too busy enjoying his favourite role as a genial, kindly gentleman to notice as the woman slipped photos from inside her coat into a large brown handbag strapped across her chest. He patted her shoulder. 'Never mind, madam. No damage done. Accidents happen. Get yourself a nice cup of tea and forget the whole thing.'

Libby mopped spilled coffee. 'Max. Did you see? That woman grabbed some of the prints.'

'Really? I was looking at Wendlebury. Got to admire the man. He's quite an operator.' He handed Libby another paper towel. 'The woman's not just clumsy, then.'

Libby nudged him. 'Don't let her leave.'

Max winked, covered the ground in a few long strides and caught up with the culprit, just as Wendlebury turned away. Max grabbed the woman's elbow. 'Not so fast. You've got a bit of explaining to do.'

Marina, Exham's most prolific gossip, had migrated to the cafe area, well away from the clear-up operation. Libby murmured in her ear, 'Do you know that woman?'

Marina's tinkly laugh rose above the hubbub in the hall. 'Of course, I do, darling, she lives in Wells. Jemima Bakewell. Recognise her from years ago, when I was teaching.'

'At the same school?'

'No. Come to think of it, I don't believe we ever had a proper conversation. She taught Classics. Dresses the part, don't you think? A spinster, of course.' Marina drifted away, losing interest and heading for Chesterton Wendlebury.

Max steered the woman towards Libby.

It was true she didn't appear to care much for fashion. Short iron grey hair, a small but conspicuous moustache, sensible brogues and a thick brown jacket stretched almost to bursting across her chest, did nothing for the woman's appearance. Her nails were broken and discoloured. *A gardener, perhaps.*

She shook Max's hand from her elbow with an irritated shrug but made no attempt to move away. Nevertheless, he positioned himself between the teacher and the door. 'Stealing photos? A teacher? Pillar of the establishment? I suggest you explain before we mention it to the community support workers. Luckily for you, they're busy helping to clean up your mess.'

The woman inspected every inch of Max, from the top of his head to the soles of his shoes, snorted her disapproval and turned away to focus on Libby. The fluffy elderly woman act had disappeared, the experienced teacher far too shrewd a judge of character to try it with either Max or Libby. 'I've seen you before, young lady. Now, where was it? I never forget a face.' She pursed her lips. 'I know, you were selling chocolates at the County Show.'

Chocolates. Oh, no. Libby gasped. She'd forgotten about the meeting in Bath. She was going to be horribly late.

As panic set in, Libby's phone trilled. She scrambled to find it at the bottom of her bag, extricated it and detached an old, fluffy mint from the screen. A message waited.

You haven't forgotten the appointment with Jumbles, have you?
Mandy.

Libby swore under her breath. Even if she left right now, she'd still be late, and she'd miss the chance to find out more about Miss Bakewell and the photographs.

She hit the buttons on her phone. 'Mandy, this is your big moment. I'm stuck here and I need you to take my place. Use a taxi. It'll cost a fortune but I'll pay you back. Just get yourself and the chocolates to Bath as fast as you can.'

She heard Mandy take a deep breath on the other end of the phone. 'Okay, Mrs F. No worries. Will do.'

* * *

Max pointed at Miss Bakewell's bag. 'Shall we take a look at the photographs you stole?'

The woman fiddled with the strap, twisting the end round her hand. 'Photographs? What do you mean?'

Libby held out a hand. 'I saw you take pictures from the easels and hide them in your coat and transfer them to your bag. You can't deny it, so you might as well explain why you wanted them. Come on, hand them over.'

For a moment, the teacher looked ready to refuse. Neither Libby nor Max had any authority to force the issue and Libby was already looking for the police workers, when Miss Bakewell sighed, delved into the bag and handed over a small stack of prints.

'I don't believe it,' Libby muttered.

Max leaned over her shoulder. 'Glastonbury Tor. Nothing odd in that. You can see plenty of photos of the Tor in the exhibition. There are more prints of the hill than anything else.'

'That's not what I mean. Look.' Libby pointed to the child in the picture, the small face dwarfed by a cloud of curly black hair, whipped to a thatch by the wind. 'That's the little girl I met on the hill.'

Miss Bakewell muttered, under her breath, 'So, it's not her, after all.'

'That's the child I met.'

The woman laughed in a high pitched voice, sounding on the verge of hysteria. 'It's all a silly mistake. Just a photograph. Not what I thought, at all.'

She made a grab for the print but Libby whisked it away. 'The photograph was taken recently. Look at the date. Oh—'

Max said, 'Now what's the matter?'

'I found that necklace on top of the Tor. I'm sure of it. The photo's dated June the twelfth last year, and the little girl's wearing the beads round her neck.'

Max rounded on the teacher. 'You'd better tell us why you took the photos. Otherwise, we'll be tempted to give them to the police; they're private property, you know. I expect you'd rather not be charged with theft.'

The woman folded her arms, scowling, but said nothing.

Max flipped through the pile. 'Most of these date back a long time. To the late sixties, I'd guess.'

'You're right.' Libby pointed. 'Look at the clothes on that couple.' The two people in the photograph, smiling at the camera, were unmistakable hippies, all long hair and necklaces.

Libby gasped. 'There's the necklace again. Look, Max, it's in the old photos as well.'

6

THE NECKLACE

Max pulled three chairs round a table and introduced Libby. Jemima Bakewell shot him a look fierce enough to curdle milk and spoke to Libby. 'Very well. I can see you're a sensible woman, Mrs Forest, so I'll explain. I found the necklace many years ago. I should have handed it in, but I didn't. I became rather fond of it.'

Libby frowned. Was she confessing to jewellery theft? It seemed unlikely.

The woman clenched her hands until the knuckles turned white. 'I assure you, young woman, it's true. I went for a walk one day, found the necklace on the Tor, liked it, popped it in my pocket and forgot about it.' She rubbed her nose. 'No one reported it missing. I would have returned it at once, if so. I'd no idea the beads had historical importance until, several weeks later, I emptied my pockets, ready to send the coat to be cleaned, and looked at the necklace more carefully.'

She swallowed and Libby frowned, confused. *She's lying, but why?* 'What do you mean by historical significance?' she asked.

'I'm a teacher of Classics. I've devoted many years to the study of ancient texts. In fact, my treatise on a comparison between the

Iron Age in Britain and the later Roman civilisation was excep-
tionally well received.' Libby nodded, trying to look impressed.
Max sighed and tapped an impatient finger on his knee, but
Libby glared, sending a signal to let the woman talk.

Miss Bakewell gained in confidence as she explained her
work. 'In my paper, I point out the importance of certain items of
jewellery to early settlers. The necklace is a case in point. It would
have formed part of the grave furniture of a high status woman,
in 250BC.' The teacher broke off. 'That's right, Mrs Forest. You
may well gasp. Those beads date back more than 2,000 years.
Archaeologists must have discovered them when they explored
the remains of the Glastonbury Lake Village settlement.' Her
neck turned pink. 'I should have handed the necklace in to the
authorities but I'd grown fond of the beads and no one seemed to
know about them.'

The fingers of one of Miss Bakewell's hands scratched at the
back of the other until Libby feared she might draw blood.

'What was so special about the beads?'

'Special?' The woman looked down, snatched her hands apart
and gripped the seat of her chair. 'Oh, just their age, of course.'
The attempt at nonchalance wouldn't fool a child. 'That was all.
They're important because they're so old, but no one was looking
for them. I thought I could keep them safe but a few weeks ago, I
heard the University was planning another excavation at the site.
I decided to hand them back, but...'

'But you lost them?'

Miss Bakewell cleared her throat. 'I – I took a walk up the Tor,
for old times' sake, and I wore the beads. They're threaded on a
piece of wire, not gold or silver, so they don't count as Treasure
Trove. The wire was old and thin and I suppose it must have
broken because when I returned home, I'd lost the beads.' She
spread her hands and sighed.

Libby said, 'As a matter of fact, I have them.'

Miss Bakewell's head flew up, eyelids stretched wide, jaw slack.

'Yes, I found them on the Tor.' *That wiped the sanctimonious expression off your face.* 'Of course,' Libby added, 'I'll return them to the proper owner when I find out who that is. If there's a new excavation, I can hand them in myself.' From the corner of her eye she saw the flash of a grin on Max's face.

Miss Bakewell scraped her chair back, grasped the handbag to her chest and took a step towards the door.

'Wait.' Libby took her arm. 'We haven't finished.'

'No, no. I have to go.' The woman's hand was trembling. 'Here's my address.' She shook off Libby's hand, scribbled on a scrap of paper, and threw the note down on the muddle of photographs. With a surprising turn of speed, she shuffled across the room and out of the door, leaving Libby standing.

Max reached for the address and whistled. 'She's quite a character.'

'She didn't think much of you,' Libby pointed out, 'and finding out I have those beads spooked her. Do you think anything she told us was true?'

'Parts of it. I reckon she made up most of the story for our benefit, probably because she's ashamed of taking the beads. I wonder where she really found them?' Max rubbed his hands. 'Let me have a look at them when we get back to Exham. Don't you love it when peculiar things happen? The Case of the Ancient Beads. That's something else for Ramshore and Forest, Detectives Extraordinaire, to investigate, don't you think?'

'I think it's all very suspicious. The man who photographed people wearing the beads died just one day before he shows the photos. It gives me the creeps. D'you think she knew him?'

Max's eyes glittered. 'We need to learn a bit more about those beads. Miss Bakewell said they came from an excavation and I'm tempted to believe that part of the story. The dig must be documented.'

'I know how we can find out more about Somerset's past.'

Max closed his eyes for a beat and groaned. 'Oh no. Definitely not. I'm not going anywhere near the local history society. I've been there once, and that was more than enough. Those women terrify me.'

'It's the best place to start. They know absolutely everything about Somerset.'

He was shaking his head. 'When Marina Sellworthy gives me the once-over I feel like a grubby and unimportant fossil from Kilve beach, and the rest of your history society friends are the biggest gossips in the West Country.'

'What do you have to hide? Are you telling me you can pull the wool over the eyes of international criminals, but you're too chicken to face the history society?'

'That's about right. A man can only withstand so much.'

'OK, I'll talk to them. There's a meeting in a couple of days, and I still provide the cakes.' Libby gathered up the photos. 'That was Marina's fault, by the way. She nabbed me about a week after I arrived, almost as though she was lying in wait. She persuaded me it would provide good advertising for my business. She can be very persuasive, and once I'd agreed it got harder to back out.'

'What flavour are you offering this time?'

'Cardamom and ginger. Tempted?'

Max grimaced. 'Sounds good, but not great enough to get me in that room. You might save me a slice, but I'll leave the society to you. I'll do some internet searches, and we can compare notes. First, though, we'd better return the photos Miss Bakewell left behind.'

Max stopped talking. She'd seen that look on his face before. 'Max? What are you cooking up?'

He took the pile of photos from Libby's hands. 'There's no hurry. We'll hand these prints over to John Williams' estate in a couple of days, but first, let's have another look at them. Maybe we'll see why they mattered so much to Miss Bakewell. I don't buy the historically valuable ancient beads story. It's not as if the police were on her trail for stealing them forty years ago.'

'You're right. She kept glancing at the photos while we were talking, as though she saw something she didn't want us to notice. I don't suppose it will hurt to keep them for a while.'

'Joe told me John Williams was single and lived alone, so there's no wife or kids wanting the photos for sentimental reasons.'

The hall had emptied, visitors at last persuaded to leave, to embellish their stories at home. Max slipped the pictures inside his jacket. 'We can't study these photos properly here. Are you free tomorrow?'

'It depends how Mandy got on this afternoon. I had to send her to Jumbles with the chocolate samples. They've talked about stocking our products, but if the meeting went horribly wrong I might need to build bridges.'

'That girl could sell nuts to Brazil if she set her mind to it. I'd like to be a fly on the wall when the Jumbles staff see her tattoos. Isn't it an old-fashioned business?'

'That's what bothers me, though their marketing girl sounded younger than I'd expected. I'd better get back home and prepare for the worst. Fingers crossed, see you tomorrow.'

* * *

Libby walked into the kitchen and her jaw dropped. 'Is that really you?' Mandy had brushed her hair until it shone. A demure hair band held the long side out of her eyes and hid most of the shaved area. She'd dabbed a subtle hint of pink blusher on her cheeks and removed most of the facial nuts and bolts, leaving only two or three earrings in each ear. Even the skull tattoo had disappeared; a fake, as Libby suspected. She recognised the pink silk shirt and pencil skirt, though. 'Are you wearing my clothes?'

Mandy swore, kicked off a pair of six inch Jimmy Choo's, the only pair of designer shoes Libby owned, and rubbed a bright red spot on her toe joint. 'Blimey, how do you wear these babies, Mrs F? They're giving me bunions.'

'Those shoes are strictly 'car to bar.' I've never tried to walk any distance in them. I just tottered across the road, sat down for dinner, and limped back to the car. Best with tights and some of those gel pads, by the way, for future reference.'

The shoes hadn't seen the light of day for years. Trevor, Libby's late husband, hadn't frequented bars. At least, she amended, he hadn't taken Libby to them. She'd recently realised she hadn't known Trevor at all, for under his respectable insurance salesman front, he'd been part of a web of fraud. His role had been laundering money through property deals.

Libby winced, remembering some of the lies he'd told.

Mandy was talking. 'Does that mean I get to wear the shoes again?'

'A little out of character for a Goth, aren't they?'

'I suppose. Anyway, I don't wear tights. Well, not those flesh coloured things.' Mandy's legwear was restricted to thick black tights. 'My toes are all, like, screwed up. Look at them.' She hoisted a bare foot on to the tabletop.

Libby shrieked. 'Don't do that. I'll lose my five star food hygiene certificate.'

'Only if an inspector happens to look in the window, and if

they're snooping about at this time of night, we'll call Max's son, grumpy Detective Sergeant Joe.'

Libby shooed Mandy out of the kitchen into the living room, wiping the table with Dettol on the way. The girl stood in the hall, hopping from one bare foot to the other. 'Don't you want to know how I got on, then?'

'I'm beside myself. Judging by your face, it went well.'

'They loved me, Jumbles did. Ate all the chocs, told me I did you credit, and said you were to give me a raise.'

'Oh, yeah?'

'Maybe not the last bit. But they've put in an order. Look.'

Mandy extracted a crumpled sheet of paper from her bag. A column of figures marched down the page and Libby whistled. 'This is easily the biggest order we've had yet.'

'It's not just for now, either. They want to try these out for starters, and if they sell, they want a repeat every month.'

'Mandy!' Libby collapsed onto the sofa, infuriating her marmalade cat. Fuzzy stalked away and slunk upstairs to hide in the airing cupboard.

'Can we do it? Fulfil the order, I mean?'

Dates and preparation times swirled round Libby's head. She sat up, taking a deep, steadying breath. 'Of course, we can. Now, I'll need your help. I've got a proposition. I've been meaning to talk to Frank about setting up an apprenticeship, and if he agrees—'

'And he always agrees with you – ever since you saved the business—'

'If he agrees, I think you'd be a great apprentice.'

'What? You mean, like, official? With qualifications and everything?'

'Absolutely.'

Mandy whooped, threw her arms in the air and jigged round

the room, giggling. At last, breathless, she flopped backwards over the arm of a chair, leaving her bare feet dangling.

'When do I start? Frank's taken on a couple of new girls, so he won't mind me moving across to the chocolate side of the business.'

'In a week, and only if Frank goes along with it. That'll give us time to get the paperwork done.'

Libby darted back to the kitchen, retrieved a bottle of chilled New Zealand Chardonnay from the fridge and poured two large glasses.

'Don't gulp, sip,' She insisted as Mandy took a huge mouthful. 'We're going to be busy, supplying Jumbles as well as the bakery. Are you up for it?'

'Watch me. Oh, nearly forgot. Your iPad's been dinging. Can't you turn the noise off?'

'Haven't got around to it.' The machine was new, and Libby hadn't got to grips with it. She flipped up the cover and checked her emails, finding one from Max, headed *The Beads*. 'He's sent photos. How do I open them?'

'Just tap.' Mandy emptied her glass and broke pieces off a bar of Cadbury's Dairy Milk, giggling at Libby's horrified double take. 'Your chocs are wonderful, Mrs F, but sometimes a girl needs, like, a proper bar of chocolate.'

As the first photograph opened, Libby studied the set of amber beads arranged on a table alongside other artefacts. She compared them to the ones she'd found on the Tor. They were identical. Alongside the necklace, Libby recognised a sharpened stone as a spear head. Max had added a note.

Found the photo online. If your beads are the same, it seems they came from an excavation near the Tor about forty years ago.

Libby smiled. Miss Bakewell had a few more questions to answer.

Max's second photo showed the Tor rising from a mist that ended just below St Michael's Tower, blocking out half the hill.

Libby said, 'The Tor looked like that when Bear and I were there.'

'Spooky,' Mandy said. 'Makes you shiver.'

7

2,000 YEARS

'Did you bring the necklace?' Max asked.

Libby and Mandy cradled mugs of coffee in Max's living room, while Bear stretched across as many feet as possible, grunting with pleasure. Libby placed her mug out of reach of the dog's tail and unzipped a small pocket in her handbag, pulling out a silk jewellery pouch that once contained a silver brooch. The amber stones felt warm against her skin. 'I've been terrified of losing them. I kept moving them around, hiding them in different places. In the end, I decided my bag's the safest place. I never go anywhere without it.'

Max agreed. 'It would take a better man than me to part a woman from her handbag.' Libby laid the beads on the coffee table.

'More than 2,000 years,' Mandy murmured. 'You wouldn't know it. They just look old and dusty, really.'

Max had spent the previous evening googling amber beads. He shared his findings. 'Amber's a strange medium. It's actually tree resin, compressed for hundreds of years. Sometimes, it traps insects or flowers, preserving them inside the amber for ever.'

Mandy giggled. 'Or until someone takes the DNA and makes dinosaurs. Like in Jurassic Park.'

Max grinned. 'I'm not sure the science of that idea holds water, but amber's been valued as a precious stone for hundreds of years. It's even thought to have healing properties.'

'I'm not surprised folk are fascinated.' Libby picked up the beads and with a sigh, slid them back into the silk pouch, zipping them in the side of her bag. 'I wish I could hang on to them but I suppose I should find the real owner and hand them back. At least they aren't part of a hoard of gold or diamonds, or Miss Bakewell would really be in trouble.'

She laid Max's *Myths and Legends* book on the table. 'I was up all night reading this. Glastonbury seems to have as many legends as ancient Greece.'

Mandy grabbed it, skimming the text. 'Well, the Tor's pretty cool, with that old ruin on top. St Michael's Tower,' she read. 'Never knew that was its name.' She pointed to a sticky note. 'What's all this about a curse?'

'It keeps cropping up.' Libby took the book and thumbed through the pages, pointing to other marked areas. 'Here, you see, and on this page. Look. Amber beads figure in the tales of King Arthur and Guinevere. Guinevere was King Arthur's young wife, but she fell in love with Lancelot, one of the twelve knights. According to the story, he travelled far and wide searching for the Holy Grail, and on the way he found a dozen 'perfect gems' which he gave to the beautiful Queen. She hid them from her husband, for fear he'd suspect her love for Lancelot, but forgot where she'd left them.'

'You'd think she'd take care of a present like that.' Mandy put in.

Remembering something, Libby scanned her notes. 'Look, she was only a teenager. Not even as old as you. I suppose girls were as forgetful then as they are now.' Mandy made a face. 'Present company excepted,' Libby added.

'Are you going to finish the story?' Max tapped a foot, impatient. Mandy rolled her eyes at Libby and mouthed, 'Men.'

'I saw that,' Max said.

Libby went on, 'One day, the beads appeared on a golden platter at dinner. Guinevere, frightened one of her household knew of her secret love and planned to inform the King, made up a story about a child finding them at the foot of a great hill. King Arthur believed her and ruled they must be kept at Glastonbury for ever. Because Guinevere lied to her husband, the story goes, bad luck would fall on anyone who touched the beads.'

Max looked from Libby to Mandy and laughed. 'I wish you could see your faces. Anyone would think you believed all this mumbo-jumbo.'

'Of course, we don't,' Libby said. 'It's just a legend. Good story, though.'

Mandy interrupted. 'So, who put the beads on the serving platter?'

'Doesn't say in the records. Someone knew about the affair with Lancelot and wanted to cause trouble. Even in Arthur's court, there were arguments and jealousies. Maybe one of her ladies wanted Lancelot for herself. Rivalry's inevitable, I think, where people live close together.'

'Like Exham on Sea?' Mandy suggested.

Max laughed, but Libby glanced at her bag, thinking about the beads. Trouble seemed to surround them, even now.

'Libby, you've gone quiet.'

'Sorry. I was thinking about jealousy and quarrels, and bad luck.'

Mandy's eyes were round. 'What do you mean?'

Libby gave a short laugh. 'I'm not sure, really, except that John

Williams took photographs of people wearing the beads and now he's dead.'

* * *

Mandy pulled on a jacket, ready to leave for a shift at the bakery. 'It's so unfair. You two can carry on drinking coffee and sleuthing, while I'm slaving in the bakery. Those new girls Frank brought in are so-o-o slow.'

'Help Frank train them up, so you can start that apprenticeship.'

Mandy mounted her bike. 'Can't wait. Don't uncover the murderer before I get back, will you?'

'Tell you what,' Libby said. 'We'll invite Max for dinner and talk more, then.'

Mandy wobbled in a circle, narrowly missing the trunk of an old ash tree as Bear tried to lick her ankles. 'By the way, what's on the menu?'

'Sticky spiced chicken. It's already in the fridge, at home. We'll just need rice. Bring Steve, if you like.'

'Young love,' Max murmured, hauling the dog indoors and kicking the door shut in one practised movement. 'I wonder how long it'll last.'

'Steve's leaving for music college in a few months. Things may fizzle out, especially if Mandy's busy with the apprenticeship. I'd be sorry, though. They're very happy.'

'At their age, they'll be changing partners every few months. Didn't you have plenty of boyfriends when you were young?'

Libby threw a ball for Bear to hide hot cheeks. 'Not really. Trevor sort of took me over, when we met. He was very persistent.'

'And he bullied you?'

'Not at first. A little, maybe, later,' she admitted. In fact, towards the end of their marriage, her husband had convinced Libby she was stupid and ugly. He kept up a daily barrage of criticism: her clothes were too tight, her hair a mess and her legs ugly and fat. When he died, a weight lifted from Libby's shoulders.

She recognised, with hindsight, how Trevor had controlled everything she did. Once he'd gone, Libby vowed to take charge of her own future, and wasted no time in leaving London for Exham on Sea. As soon as she arrived in town, she set about building a new life making cakes and chocolates.

When she'd uncovered Trevor's involvement in the series of financial frauds Max was investigating, Libby was mortified.

'Talking of Trevor,' Max said, 'which is a subject we try to avoid, I've got a meeting in London soon, to pull together the threads of money laundering in Leeds.' Libby snorted.

'What?'

'Sorry. Laundry. Threads. You know. It seemed funny for a moment.' She swallowed. 'I get nervous when we talk about Trevor.'

'There's no need for you to feel bad. Your husband had a portfolio of houses bought with funny money. You didn't. You've done nothing illegal. Be patient a while longer. I'm hoping we can wind the whole business up soon.'

'The sooner the better.' Libby had an idea. 'I need some fresh air. D'you fancy a walk? Let's pick up Shipley from Marina and go out to the cliffs at High Down.'

Shipley's high pitched yelp echoed from inside Marina's house. As the door opened, the springer spaniel bounded out, whining with excitement, nails clattering on the wood floor. Libby grabbed his collar and guided him back into the house. Marina seemed ill at ease, with flushed cheeks and untidy hair. 'Are you all right?' Libby asked.

'Fine, I'm fine.' Someone coughed inside the house, and Libby had to bite her cheeks to keep from laughing. That cough didn't belong to Henry Sellworthy.

'Is it an awkward time?' Libby's tone was innocent. Her friend appeared to be conducting the affair in her own home, right under her husband's nose.

Marina's eyes flashed, but she beckoned Libby to come inside. 'Actually, Chester's here. We're going over a few business details.'

Business? Libby shrugged. It was nothing to do with her. 'I won't come in. I'm wearing wellies, ready for a walk on High Down. We're taking Bear and I thought Shipley might like to come.'

'We?' Marina peered round Libby.

Max stuck his head out of the Land Rover and waved. 'Hi, Marina. Fancy a run?'

'No, thank you.' Her voice crackled with ice. She raised an eyebrow at Libby and murmured, 'You two spend a lot of time together, these days. Still, you're a free woman, now Trevor's gone.'

Libby started. 'You sound as though you knew my husband? Had you met?'

Marina waved a hand vaguely. 'Oh, just the once. You were on holiday in the area, I believe, and Trevor took a few hours to discuss business with Chester – some boring insurance details about damage to one of Pritchard's business premises. I think he said you took the children to a matinee at the Hippodrome.'

'Yes, Trevor worked on the Pritchards' account.' She remembered that day, halfway through their holiday in Exham. Ali had begged for them all to go to Bristol, to the ballet, but Trevor refused. He said he couldn't bear to sit through an afternoon of dancing, but he'd take them all out to dinner as compensation.

Marina had never mentioned knowing Trevor. That was odd, but perhaps she didn't want Libby to know more about her involvement with Chesterton Wendlebury. That seemed to be far more than just a business relationship.

Lately, Libby had discovered her husband had hidden some rather unsavoury business connections from her, but Marina would know nothing about all that.

She smiled at her friend. She wouldn't discuss her relationship with Max. That would give Marina even more ammunition for tittle-tattle. 'What about it, Shipley? Ready for a walk?'

At the magic words, a frenzy of excitement sent Shipley scurrying to the back of the house to find his lead.

Marina followed, a cloud of perfume drifting in her wake. Libby recognised the scent. *Poison;* a heady, glamorous perfume.

Marina produced her parting remark. 'You know it's going to rain, don't you?'

Shipley dragged Libby out to the Land Rover, Bear barked a greeting, the spaniel piled in the back, Libby jumped in the front and Max drove off, squealing the tires to make Marina roll her eyes.

'There's something going on between Marina and Chesterton Wendlebury,' Libby said. 'Do you think she's about to leave Henry?'

'And deprive herself of his pension? Not likely.'

'Wendlebury's a rich man. He could look after her.'

Max shot an odd look in her direction. 'Rich on paper. He makes a good job of being the local squire, I grant you, but I've a feeling things aren't all they seem.'

'I've never quite trusted him,' Libby confessed, 'and he seems to have been one of Trevor's rather shady contacts.' Libby had looked into a house her husband owned in Leeds, and found he bought it on behalf of Pritchards.

'You don't trust anyone.' Max was brisk.

'Not surprising, since my husband turned out to be involved in some dubious deals.' Libby stole a sideways glance at Max. What did he mean, she didn't trust anyone?

'Don't look so worried.' He said. 'In our business, it doesn't hurt to be cautious.'

'Our business?'

'Private investigation. Come on, Libby, we've talked about it before. You've got a nose for things that don't add up and a logical brain. I've been trained in undercover financial research. I'm not suggesting you ditch the cakes and chocolate. You've got a great business going there, and we're never going to make a fortune as private eyes, but we're good partners.'

Libby's heart pumped so fast she thought Max would hear it

over the rumble of the engine. She took a deep breath. He meant business partners, of course. It was Mandy's fault Libby felt so unsettled. She'd suggested he cared, just because they went to the exhibition in his posh new Jaguar.

Libby pulled a map out of the pocket of the car door and pretended to study the route to High Down, while she let her flaming cheeks cool. 'Let me think about it, Max. The chocolate business is just beginning to take off, and I've asked Mandy to do a proper apprenticeship. When that's going well, maybe...'

'Let's face it,' he went on, 'we're already working together. Why not make it official? You know, business cards, a website and a bit of mouth to mouth advertising. That's all I'm suggesting.'

'But what happens if we're in the middle of an investigation, and you suddenly disappear to South America for work? How can I trust you, when you keep things from me?' Max turned and stared.

Libby grabbed the wheel. 'Look where you're going.'

'I'm not the one who ran their car into the ditch.'

'I've only done it once. Don't change the subject. The point is, how can I work with a partner who takes off without a word and never tells me where he's going?'

Max let the silence draw on. When he spoke again, he sounded thoughtful. 'I suppose you've got a point, but I won't be doing consultancy work for ever.'

Libby swallowed hard, battling to keep her breathing steady as Max pulled through a gate and drove along a rutted path towards the cliffs. As the Land Rover drew to a halt, Bear and Shipley whined and drooled with excitement. Max jumped out, threw open the doors and shooed the dogs onto the Downs, where the first few drops of rain heralded Marina's promised rainstorm.

* * *

The rain drove hard across High Down, but neither of the dogs cared a jot. Libby pulled up the hood of her new parka, zipped the collar and strode on, enjoying the rain against her face. In London, she'd always carried an umbrella, terrified of a sudden storm causing her unruly hair to frizz, but she'd learned to love a good downpour.

To her surprise, Max took her arm. 'Sorry if I upset you,' he murmured.

'You didn't,' she lied, startled.

He squeezed her arm. 'Come on, let's look round the old fort.'

For half an hour, they explored the ruined buildings. Shipley raced in and out of the wartime pillbox while Bear investigated interesting holes in the ground and chased imaginary rabbits.

'The rain's getting worse,' Max pointed out. 'Maybe we should go. Am I really invited to this sticky chicken dinner tonight, or have I blown my chances?'

A sudden burst of barking interrupted him. Bear hovered at the edge of the cliff.

'Can you smell another rabbit?' Libby waded through muddy puddles on the path. As she reached Bear's vantage point, Shipley appeared behind her, keen to see what Bear was doing. He brushed past Libby, just as she raised a foot to step over another puddle.

Caught off balance, she tripped and fell, rolling down the steep slope, scrabbling to clutch at tufts of grass and wildflower stems.

'Libby!' Max was too far away to help as Libby slid over the edge of the cliff. After a long moment, she landed with a thud that squeezed every ounce of air from her lungs. Her head connected with something hard. *So that's what it means to see stars.*

For a moment, lights swirled in front of her eyes before darkness descended.

* * *

She opened her eyes. A wide ledge further down the cliff face had broken her fall. Max was at the cliff edge, looking down, horror etched on every line of his face.

'Libby,' he called. 'Can you hear me? Are you OK?'

Libby tried to lift her right hand but it wouldn't move. Her wrist seemed to twist at an odd angle and it ached. She tried her left hand, relieved to find it uninjured. She used it to wave.

Max called, 'I'm on my way. I'll get a rope from the car.'

'No, don't come. You'll fall too.'

As she shouted, Bear jumped down from the top of the cliff and licked Libby's face. 'Get off, Bear. I'm quite all right.'

She lifted her head and discovered she wasn't quite all right. Her head hurt.

Moving as little as possible, she stole a glance over the ledge and shivered at the drop. She'd been close to falling the full height of the cliff. Bear stood between Libby and the drop and she pulled his warm body closer. 'You're a clever old dog. I'm glad you're here.'

'Hold tight.' Max was back. 'I've tied the rope to a tree. I'm coming down.' Seconds later, he joined her on the ledge. 'I'm getting too old for this.' He held out the end of the rope. 'Now, tie it round your waist, in case you slip. It'll stop you falling further.'

Libby fumbled, trying to tie a knot with one shaky hand. Max's fingers were warm on hers as he took the rope. 'Here, let me do it. I was a boy scout, you know. Knots are my thing.'

He secured the rope around Libby's waist. 'That's a bowline, I believe. I hope you're impressed.' He slid an arm round her shoulders. 'What's the matter with your hand?'

'I hurt my wrist.'

'Anything else?'

'A bit of a headache. Nothing to worry about.'

Side by side, they looked up at the climb. 'Can you make it, or should I ring for the coastguard?'

'Don't you dare. I don't want my picture in the paper.'

'You're as white as a sheet. Is your wrist broken?'

'Only a sprain, I think.' Libby cradled her right hand with her left. 'It only hurts if I move it.'

'I suggest you don't move it.'

With Max's arm round her shoulders, keeping her safe, Libby felt light headed. Overcome with relief at not falling to her death, she giggled and found she couldn't stop. Even Max was infected, his shoulders shaking with laughter. Bear remained on the ledge, patient, waiting for his two foolish humans to calm down, while Shipley scampered back and forth at the top of the cliff, thrilled by so much excitement, barking at the top of his lungs.

Max made his hands into a cup for Libby's foot and hoisted her to his shoulders. Her head reached a little above the lip of the cliff. 'Right,' Max said. 'On three.'

He placed both hands firmly on her bottom and gave a mighty shove that sent her up and over the top, clinging on with her good hand as she scrambled, one knee following the other, onto the grass above.

Bear leaped up, making easy work of the jump. Max heaved himself up on the rope and joined Libby where she lay on her back.

'Take me home,' she begged. 'I think I've had enough fresh air for one day.'

9

STICKY SPICED CHICKEN

Miss Bakewell's stolen photographs decorated one wall of Libby's living room. Mandy, Max and Libby, her wrist tightly bandaged, scrutinised each picture in turn.

'We know these were taken by John Williams,' Libby said, 'but why did Miss Bakewell try to steal them?'

Mandy walked down the line, head on one side. 'The same people keep cropping up. Look, there's a couple of, like, hippies, I guess. All droopy moustaches and afro hair. These must be their girlfriends.' She squealed. 'Wow. Sick clothes.'

'You can talk.' Libby gestured at Mandy's latest tattoo, a lurid design representing a skull with angel's wings. 'I hope that's not permanent, by the way.'

Mandy tossed her head. 'I'm not daft.'

Libby returned to the photos. 'Caftans, tight purple loons and flowery shirts with enormous sleeves were high fashion in the sixties, Mandy. You know, Carnaby Street, the Rolling Stones, miniskirts the first time round...'

'Yeah. I've seen the retro stuff, like, a million times. The Beatles, Sergeant Pepper, Hari Krishna, psychedelic drugs, frizzy hair...'

'No proper hair straighteners in those days. Girls used steam irons on their hair, so most of the time it was pretty much as nature intended.'

Max, tired of their discussion of sixties culture, studied a photo at the end of the row. It showed a girl wearing a tiny skirt and a wide-brimmed hat. 'If I'm not very much mistaken, that's our Jemima Bakewell, in her youth.'

'Never.' Libby leaned close and squinted. 'Are you sure? I mean, look at all that lovely brown hair. I suppose, if you picture that face with short grey hair and a pair of spectacles, it could be her.'

Mandy sniffed. 'You said Miss Bakewell needed make-up and a decent haircut. She looks cool in the photo.'

'Deteriorated over the years,' Libby sighed. 'Happens to us all, as you'll find out soon enough, Mandy.'

Bear lay on his back, wriggling, demanding attention. With his three favourite humans in the room at the same time, surely at least one could talk to him. Mandy gave in, squatted down and scratched his stomach while Max and Libby focused on the photos. Max sucked his teeth. 'I'm almost certain it's Miss Bakewell. See that mole on her cheek?'

He was right. The girl laughing into the camera had the teacher's mole and Libby recognised that square jaw. 'How old d'you think she was when the photo was taken? Nineteen or twenty?'

'About that, I'd guess. Let me do the sums.' Max paused. 'Yes, she must be over sixty now. I'd say that's about right.'

'It looks like she had a boyfriend. That one in the pink shirt has his arm round her. I wonder why she didn't admit to being in the picture.'

Interested, Mandy strolled back to the photos. 'Hey,' she shouted. Bear grunted, lurched to his feet and pushed his head under her arm. 'Get away, Bear. I wasn't talking to you. Look, Mrs F, she's wearing the amber beads.'

Max thumped Mandy's back. 'So she is. Well spotted. Maybe that's why she took the photos; so no one could see her with the stolen necklace.'

'Or perhaps she didn't want to be recognised. I think we need to find out more about these people; who they are and what they know about the necklace.'

Libby gasped. 'I've just realised. You see the girl behind the others? The one with long black curls half way down her back? She looks like the child on the top of the Tor.'

'Pretty girl,' said Max, 'but there were thousands of pretty girls with hot pants and long black hair in the sixties. She could be anyone.'

Libby compared the modern photo of the child with the old picture of Miss Bakewell and her companions. 'They look exactly like each other. Same hair, similar noses, and their smiles are identical. They must be related.'

'Maybe. Miss Bakewell will know, but will she tell the truth?' Max began with the first photo and pointed at each in turn. 'These people are probably all local. The photographs are taken in several different places, all near here. There's the Tor, and this one,' he said, pointing, 'shows the beach in Exham. Look, there's the lighthouse. And that's the Knoll, just outside town.'

Mandy took up the thread. 'So, they were all here together. Could they have been on holiday?'

'No, I don't reckon that's it. If that were the case, all the snapshots would be taken within a few days or weeks, but if you look carefully, you can see they're spread out across a year or more.'

His finger moved from one picture to the next. 'Here, the trees are bare, photographed in winter, but this one's taken in the summer. The trees are in leaf, there are flowers in the hedgerows and the girls are wearing thin dresses.' He hummed as he thought. 'Yes, I reckon they're students.'

'Why?'

'For one thing, they're all about the same age but they're too old to be school kids. We've agreed they look maybe nineteen or twenty. So, we've got a group of young people together for long periods of time.'

'You're right.' Mandy punched Max's shoulder, getting her revenge. 'They're all students at the same University.'

Libby added, 'Miss Bakewell was reading Classics, so I wouldn't mind betting they were at Bristol University. They award degrees in Greek and Latin.' She held up her undamaged hand in self-defence. 'And if either of you thumps me on the back, I'll empty my wine on your head. My arm's still aching.' Excitement carried her along. 'It's a starting point, at least. Would anyone at the University remember students from those days?'

Max was humming again. 'Where do you keep old newspapers?'

'In the rack, over there.' Libby pointed behind the sofa. 'Why?'

He dragged out a muddle of magazine fliers and old papers and Libby winced. Time to throw a few things out. The cottage had needed a spring clean for weeks.

Max shuffled the pile, flicking through pages, tossing them aside in a swelling flood of paper on the floor. 'Ah. Thought he looked familiar.' He folded a recent copy of the Bristol Gazette into a neat square and held it next to one of the photos. 'Look.'

Libby narrowed her eyes, trying to see a likeness. 'You're right,' she agreed. 'The boy standing next to Miss Bakewell in the photo looks like the man in the newspaper. Only much younger. Who is he?'

'A Professor Malcolm Perivale.' Apparently, he presented a paper to the Bristol Antiquarians on radiocarbon dating of bronze artefacts.' Max's eyes gleamed. 'I've seen him on television a few times. One of those arrogant, know-it-all experts who wear three piece suits and cravats. He's an archaeologist, but I suspect it's a good while since he got his own hands dirty.'

'And what's more,' Libby read from the paper. 'He's worked at the University for years. I think we should pay him a visit as soon as possible. He might be able to tell us more about these students and I bet he knows all about the necklace.'

'That's all very well,' Mandy complained, 'but you promised us sticky spiced chicken for dinner, Steve will be here in a minute and I'm starving.'

Libby waved her bandaged wrist in the air and Mandy groaned. 'I'd better start the rice.'

* * *

Late next morning, Frank, the owner of Brown's bakery and now Libby's partner in the chocolate business, loaded boxes into her Citroen. 'Thanks for offering to deliver the cake.'

Libby hovered. 'Take care. The icing's still soft.'

Frank pointed at her arm. 'Can you manage?'

'No problem. It doesn't even hurt any more, and the headache disappeared after a good night's sleep. I feel a fraud wearing this bandage on my wrist. Anyway, I'm glad to help. We can't leave a customer without a cake for her son's birthday party. I hope she got the ice cream organised.'

A frantic late-night phone call, from the harassed, forgetful parent of a five year old with his heart set on a Spiderman cake, led to a rapid flurry of design and icing in the bakery.

'Good job we weren't too busy. I'll get this over to – er...' Libby consulted the scrap of paper Frank had thrust into her hand. 'To little Ernest. Ouch. Who calls their child Ernest?'

'Think your rust bucket will make it?' Frank leaned in at the car window. 'Sounds a bit rough.'

'It always sounds rough. Alan Jenkins at the garage keeps it going for me. Mind you,' Libby let in the clutch with a loud screech, 'he keeps trying to sell me a new one. I think there are at least a few thousand miles left in this old thing.'

With a wave, she drove off on the mission of mercy.

Ernest's mother, hair escaping from an elastic band on the top of her head, tiny infant in one arm and smelly nappy in the other hand, looked as exhausted as only a mother with young children can. Libby juggled the cake one handed into the kitchen and made a space on the table, elbowing aside a jumble of socks, Babygros, muslin squares and vests.

The trip to Bristol gave Libby time to call on Professor Malcolm Perivale, the man in Miss Bakewell's stolen photos. Max was free to accompany her, and he'd suggested they have lunch at a restaurant in Bristol before visiting the professor. Libby tugged at her pencil skirt, hoping it wasn't too short, conscious of her mother's half remembered warnings about mutton dressed as lamb.

A schoolboy on a scooter sped around the corner, almost under her wheels, and Libby slammed on the brakes. After that, she concentrated on the road, blocking thoughts of Max from her mind.

Squeezing the car into one of the last spaces at Bristol Harbourside, she walked across the bridge, a stiff little breeze blowing hair in her eyes. Max, unusually smart in a suit and tie, waved from a table for two in the window of the restaurant. Had he dressed to impress Libby, or the professor?

Libby smoothed a lock of hair behind an ear, fingered a gold chain that hung round her neck, and took a deep breath. 'Have you been waiting long?'

'Only five minutes. I'm mixing business and pleasure. I had an appointment with a firm of auditors in Queen Square.' That explained the suit. 'Pritchards is their client.'

Pritchards. The company with Chesterton Wendlebury on the board; the one Trevor had dealings with. 'Are they as shady as we suspected?'

A waitress brought plates of food. 'I've ordered tapas, hope that's all right?'

'Lovely.' Libby ran an eye over dishes of chorizo, tortilla and seafood. 'Calamari? Terrific. Haven't had squid for ages.' She piled it onto her plate.

'Thought you'd like it. Can't bear the stuff, myself, so I'm sticking to roast peppers and ham.'

'Did the auditors tell you anything interesting about Pritchards, or are they bound to secrecy by client privilege?'

'I have ways of making companies talk.'

Libby spluttered. 'Strong arm stuff? No, I don't believe it.' Max was tall, trim and looked fit, but no match for gym bunnies in their thirties.

'Much too old for that. My leverage is more in the nature of a financial threat, if you know what I mean. Looking at the firm's tax situation, for example. Amazing how willing companies are to help, once I suggest that. You'd be surprised how many financial wizards neglect their own records.'

'I'd better keep the chocolate accounts straight, then.'

'Or bribe me with the product.' Max served garlicky shrimp to them both. 'This is good, whatever it is, though we'd better not breathe too hard on the professor. Anyway, Pritchards have a pretty complex set up. Off-shore accounts, a series of complicated financial instruments and a lot of buying and selling of shares among board members. Not illegal, unless it's used to manipulate prices on the stock market.'

'And Chesterton Wendlebury's been doing that?'

'He's certainly an active board member.'

Libby hesitated, not sure she wanted to ask the next question. 'What about Trevor? You said his name was on some documents you found. How was he involved with Pritchards?'

Max wiped sauce from his chin. 'He dealt with their insurance, all above board and open for scrutiny, but I'm afraid he was also in on some of the murkier deals.' Libby kept her eyes on her fork, moving squid from one side of the plate to the other. When she thought about Trevor and his criminal past, her stomach churned. What would she find out next? She laid her fork down, unable to eat any more.

Max changed the subject. 'Mandy seems happy. Growing up, do you think?'

Libby forced her whirling thoughts back from Trevor to her lodger. 'Steve's influence, I suspect. They spend a lot of time together. There's a gig tonight with his band. I sometimes get the impression Steve's not entirely committed to being a Goth, though, which is probably a good thing.'

'It's tough being a teenage boy, no matter how easy it looks.'

Libby glanced up. 'That sounded as though it came from the heart.'

Max smiled, but his eyes were serious. 'I wish I'd known you when we were young.'

Thrown off balance, heart racing, Libby couldn't think of a single thing to say. She waited, to see if he'd explain. Did he mean he cared about her? Was he asking for more than friendship?

Max said no more, but went on eating, avoiding her eye. Libby, suddenly tired of uncertainties, of second guessing Max's motives and wondering what he was thinking, downed a gulp of wine and plucked up every scrap of courage.

'Max, never mind Mandy and Steve.' She swallowed. 'Don't you think it's time you and I decided whether we're having a relationship?'

There, she'd said it. She clenched her hands tight under the table, so tense she could barely catch her breath, and waited.

Silence dragged on until she thought she might scream. At last, Max raised his head to look at Libby's face, unsmiling. 'Don't ask me to answer that, Libby. Not yet.'

10

PROFESSOR

Max might as well have punched her in the stomach. *I'm not going to cry.* Slowly, she unclenched her fists, looking everywhere except at him. 'It – it doesn't matter. I thought – you know – I wanted to be sure.' She took a deep breath that made her head swim. 'I was going to say we should keep things strictly business. I don't think either of us is looking for any sort of – er – arrangement.'

She was talking too fast, struggling to hide the hurt. She shrugged into her coat. 'It's time for us to meet the professor.'

Max busied himself with the bill. 'Your car or mine?'

Libby glanced at her wine glass. How much wine had she swallowed? 'Better be yours.'

'Look, Libby, let me explain—'

'There's nothing to explain. Nothing at all. Let's get going.'

The ride to the professor's house seemed interminable, the atmosphere in the car claustrophobic. Libby clenched her arms tight to her sides, pressing her knees against the passenger door, terrified Max might touch her leg. She couldn't bear him to think she'd engineered a contact.

In her head, she replayed the scene in the restaurant, each iteration more depressing than the last. She'd exposed her feelings for nothing. Max shared none of them. She shot a glance at his profile. A cheek muscle twitched, but his eyes stayed on the road.

Well, Libby could live without Max. What was it she'd said to the children, breaking the news of her move to Exham? 'I'm starting a new life. I'm going to be independent. I can make my own living.' She'd meant it, too. She didn't need a new man.

Max yanked hard on the handbrake as they arrived, climbed out of the car and walked to the professor's house. He didn't even come round to open Libby's door.

The professor appeared on the threshold of his house before they reached the halfway point on the path. His shapeless brown jacket had leather patches on the arms. Perhaps he bought it when he reached the starry heights of professorship in an attempt to look the part. Under normal circumstances, Libby would have shared a glance with Max, but today she couldn't bear to look at him.

Instead, she focused on the professor, picking up an overwhelming impression of an absent minded academic, a kind of Einstein look-alike. The man's wire-framed glasses teetered halfway up his forehead. Tufts of wispy hair stood out like an electrified white halo.

'Come in, come in,' he boomed, waving the visitors along a corridor to his study.

Stacks of students' work overflowed every chair. A globe stood in a prominent spot on a side table next to a sherry decanter, and in one corner, a glass cabinet displayed misshapen pieces of pottery and metal. Libby peeked inside, noticing chunks of iron with sharpened ends, a lump of greenish glass and something that looked like a primitive saw.

'I see you're admiring my artefacts,' the professor said, prolonging the word, emphasising every syllable, a technique most likely developed for the benefit of sleepy students. 'They're from the Glastonbury Lake Village. Over 2,000 years old. Can you imagine that?'

Libby and Max sat apart, awkward on a lumpy sofa, separated by a gap that felt as wide as Exham beach. They refused sherry, biscuits and coffee.

'So,' the professor said. 'How can I help you? Is it about the new excavations? You don't look much like the usual amateur archaeologists. No dirt under your nails.' His smile exposed a gap between the front teeth.

'We wanted to ask you about John Williams. He was at University with you.'

The smile faded. 'Haven't seen him for years. Heard he topped himself. Read it in the papers. The man was a waste of space. Huh.'

He downed a glass of sherry in one gulp and poured another. 'Sure you won't?' He waved the glass. Not the man's first drink of the day, judging by the bulbous nose and red cheeks. Libby turned towards Max, remembered they weren't speaking and looked down at her hands.

Max said, 'Some of his photographs were in a local exhibition. Jemima Bakewell was there.'

The professor frowned. 'Was she, by George? Shouldn't have been.' His mouth snapped shut, as though he'd said more than he should.

What did he mean by that? Libby leaned forward, elbows on her knees. The man was half drunk. She intended to take advantage of the fact and find out everything she could. 'Tell me about Jemima Bakewell and John Williams and the others. You were friends, weren't you?'

'Used to be. Not any more. Had a falling out, you know, over some stupid business, back when we were young. Huh. Something to do with Jemima's beads. She lost 'em, accused us of stealing the things.' The professor waved a hand. 'Can't remember the sordid details. Far too long ago. Went our separate ways. Haven't seen 'em since then.'

'Those beads. Miss Bakewell said she found them.'

'Maybe she did. They're fine examples of Iron Age amber. We were just students, then.' His laugh turned into a cough. 'Seen more beads than I could shake a stick at since. Nothing like the first time, though. Beauties, they were.' The professor wiped his face on a large blue handkerchief. 'Hot, today. Must be a storm coming.'

'When did you last see Miss Bakewell?'

He folded the handkerchief into a neat square and tucked it with care into his jacket pocket. 'Not since we were students.'

Max raised an eyebrow. 'But you only live a few miles apart. You must have bumped in to each other at conferences or similar. I mean, she studies the Classics, you're an archaeologist...'

The professor's ruddy face deepened to an unhealthy purple. 'You calling me a liar? Huh!'

Max's lip twitched. He'd scored a hit. 'And the beads?'

The professor's eyelids flickered. 'Those beads. Yes.' Libby could hardly keep a straight face at the sudden grunts and exclamations. Maybe they were involuntary, like a twitch. His students must have fun with them. 'Made of amber. Know anything about amber?'

Sensing a lecture, Libby interrupted, 'I'm sure you know all the myths surrounding the beads.'

'Myths? I don't deal in myths, young lady.' The glare would silence a roomful of the rowdiest undergraduates. 'Stuff and nonsense. The beads are mentioned in the records. From the grave of a high status woman, one would imagine. Possibly stolen by vandals. Yes. Grave robbery's a taboo, you know. Always was. Some nonsense about the beads being cursed. Huh! Made up in recent years. Glastonbury's the place for myths and legends. King Arthur, lot of tosh. Good for tourism, that's all. Huh.'

'Have you been to Glastonbury lately?'

'Not since the last excavation, three, four years ago. Place is full of tourists, these days.'

Max asked, 'Where were you two days ago?'

'Me? What day was it now? Tuesday? Huh! Yes. Spent the morning in a tutorial with a student, then lunch with colleagues. Someone's leaving do. And, now, I have work, so if you'll excuse me...'

* * *

The professor poured more sherry into a crystal glass and let Libby and Max find their own way out. 'Take me back to my car,' Libby demanded.

'You've had far too much wine. I'll drive you home, and when you get a free day, we'll come back to get your car.'

Another silent drive, then, and Libby wouldn't be first to speak. After a few miles, Max broke the oppressive silence. 'What did you make of our professor? Huh!'

Libby refused to smile at the imitation.

He went on, 'I don't think he could help the twitches, but he's a pompous old fool and he didn't want to tell us anything. He's in the clear for John Williams' death, anyway. His student can put him in Bristol on the morning John Williams died.'

Libby said nothing.

Max tried again. 'Reading between the professor's lines, they made some pact never to meet again. What could have shaken them so much?'

'No idea.'

'Do you know, I think I'd like to pay another visit to our professor.'

Libby said, 'You'll have to go on your own. I'm going to the history society meeting tomorrow.'

'I'll come up on the train, then, and bring your car back.'

Libby just shrugged. She wasn't going to thank him. She never wanted to see the man again.

Max's new Jaguar drew up at her house. A lump formed in Libby's throat as Max killed the engine. 'Libby, you caught me off guard at lunch.'

'I didn't mean to embarrass you.' Libby's voice quivered.

'You deserve an explanation—'

'No need.' She had to get out of the car, right away.

Max put a hand on her arm. 'I should give you a proper answer to your question.'

'No.' She pushed him away, shoved the car door open and swung her legs out. 'No explanations, no answers. We're partners. And friends, I suppose. That's all. It's good to know where we stand.' She strode away, refusing to look back, determined Max should not see the tears that coursed down her cheeks.

11

EXHAM HISTORY SOCIETY

Next day, Libby spent far too long composing questions for the history society meeting. Her car still in Bristol, she arrived late, hampered by the need to walk with Bear's lead in one hand and a bag containing cake tins in the other. Marina opened the door, scarlet and pink scarves flying, silver bracelets clanking. 'Libby, darling, how's your wrist? And did you remember to bring the cake?'

Libby let Bear off the lead. 'Hope you don't mind Bear coming. Max is on his way to Bristol to – er – talk to an old colleague, so he left Bear with me.'

'Bear can stay in the back room. Shipley's always pleased to see him.' Marina's house, a substantial, brick built Georgian mansion, included several rooms at the rear. These, built in the days when servants were commonplace, had once served as sculleries and dairies. Now, they were perfect for dogs.

Shipley greeted Bear in Marina's back cloakroom, barking and running in circles, full of unhinged excitement. Libby sometimes wondered if the spaniel could be heading for a stroke.

The drawing room, far more elegant than the servants' quarters, buzzed with gossip. Samantha Watson stopped talking in mid-sentence as Libby entered and wrinkled her nose.

Marina's stage whisper must have been audible to everyone. 'Chief Inspector Arnold rang Samantha with the news.' Samantha, having divorced her ne'er-do-well husband, Ned, was engaged to Chief Inspector Arnold, Joe's boss.

'I'm sorry,' Libby confessed. 'I've no idea what you're talking about. What news?'

'Well,' Samantha sipped from a delicate bone china teacup, one little finger held aloft with a daintiness Libby hadn't seen since she was a child at her mother's tea parties. 'The Chief Inspector told me about the explosion.'

The woman's smile could have frozen waves on Exham beach. 'He said it had something to do with a schoolteacher. Marina says you were talking to the woman at the photographic exhibition, Lizzy.'

Libby's heart lurched. She ignored the deliberate mispronunciation of her name. 'If there's something you think I should know, I'd be grateful if you'd tell me.'

'Oh, the police will talk to you soon enough, I'm sure. The Chief Inspector says everywhere you go, trouble follows.'

Libby sighed. 'Samantha, I have no idea what you're talking about. Has something happened to Miss Bakewell?'

Samantha slapped her cup so hard onto its saucer, the contents slopped onto Marina's marble topped table. She pointed a manicured finger at Libby. 'I knew you'd be involved. I wish people would mind their own business instead of poking around in local affairs...'

'Do calm down, Samantha,' Marina broke in. 'I'm sure Libby knows nothing about the explosion.'

Libby lost patience. 'For heaven's sake, tell me what you're talking about. What explosion, and why do you think I'm involved?'

'Well, darling, you and Max Ramshore were at the photography exhibition together, talking to that Miss Bakewell.'

'Why shouldn't I have been there? You were there, too, Marina.'

'No reason at all. I'm just explaining. According to Samantha, the inspector told her—'

'Chief Inspector,' Samantha put in.

Marina sighed. 'Chief Inspector Arnold said Miss Bakewell has been involved in an accident.'

'I'm sorry to hear that.' An accident?

The back of Libby's neck prickled. What was that nonsense about the beads and a curse? 'What kind of accident are you talking about?'

Marina was enjoying the limelight. 'Apparently, she went to see some professor. Perivale, that was the name. After she left his house, there was some sort of explosion.'

Professor Perivale's house? Libby's throat felt tight. She whispered. 'Was anyone hurt?'

'That's all we know.'

Libby's hands were clenched tight in her lap, the knuckles white. Her nails forced themselves into the palms. She stood up. 'Doesn't anyone know any more?'

Someone said, 'We might catch the local news, if we're quick,' and Marina switched on the vast television. Libby bit her lip, trying to think, but there was only one idea in her head. What if Max was there? He planned to visit the professor today. He could be hurt, or even dead.

A local reporter stood in front of a row of tall Victorian houses that had a jagged edged gap, like a missing tooth, in the centre. Libby recognised the street she'd visited yesterday.

'Police say one person has been taken to hospital, but no one else was in the house,' intoned the journalist. 'Neighbours tell us the property belongs to a Professor Perivale from Bristol University. It's believed he may be the injured man. We have no further news at this time.'

Not Max. The words hammered in Libby's head. *Max isn't dead.*

'Are you all right, Libby?' Marina's face creased with anxiety. 'You're white as a sheet.'

'I'm fine.' Libby's phone rang. She fumbled the buttons with shaking fingers as the name flashed up on the screen. *Max.* 'I have to take this.'

She stumbled to her feet and ran to the hall, as Samantha remarked, 'Really, some people are so *over-dramatic.*'

'Max, are you OK? I saw the news...'

'You've heard about the explosion, then. Don't worry, I'm fine. Miss Bakewell's pretty shaken, though. I'm about to drive her home.'

'What was she doing there? And what about the professor?'

'He's gone to hospital, but the neighbours say he was awake and talking while they put him in the ambulance.'

'Did you speak to him?'

'No, unfortunately, the explosion came a moment before I arrived. Miss Bakewell had just left. I'm hoping the shock will make her a little more forthcoming about the photographs. Could you meet us at her house in Wells? We'll be there in less than an hour. I want to find out what she was doing at the professor's house, and I think it would be better if you were there. Will you come?'

Libby looked at the phone. Max sounded stressed. No wonder. 'Yes, of course. I'll get a taxi. Lilly's Cabs are always happy to carry dogs. Max, what do you think happened?'

His voice was grim. 'I don't know, but the professor could have died. It's a coincidence, don't you think?'

Libby shivered. She dropped her phone in a pocket. The history society would have to wait. When she took a step, her legs shook so much she could hardly walk, and she sank down on to the stairs.

The adrenaline of fear ebbed away, leaving her exhausted, and she let her head drop between her knees until the faintness passed. She was still mad at Max, but at least he wasn't dead.

12

Jemima Bakewell kept a bottle of whisky in a corner cupboard in her kitchen. It took Libby only a few minutes to track it down and pour a big slug into a cup of tea, add six lumps of sugar and carry it through to the tiny sitting room, where Bear, bribed by treats, lay curled in a corner.

The retired schoolteacher pulled a plaid blanket tight round her shoulders and sipped. 'I knew something like this would happen. It's all coming horribly true.'

She looked thirty years older than last time Libby saw her.

The room was stuffed with mementos from Miss Bakewell's travels. Busts of Greek philosophers jostled with photographs showing the teacher in various locations. Libby studied them while the woman drank her tea. In one picture, Miss Bakewell wore a sun hat and waved a trowel, surrounded by the open trenches of an archaeological dig. Another showed her walking in the Greek islands, while in another she was with a group of middle-aged ladies wearing flowery skirts and cardigans, enjoying a bottle of red wine under azure skies.

Books cluttered every spare inch of space in the room. A Latin dictionary and a well-thumbed copy of the Aeneid leaned against a leather bound version of the poems of Catullus. It was clear Miss Bakewell loved her subject.

Max remained silent, letting Miss Bakewell recover from the shock of the explosion at the professor's house. He raised an eyebrow at Libby, and she nodded.

He said, 'I think it's time you told us the truth, Miss Bakewell, don't you?'

Taken aback by the sharp tone, the woman licked her lips, eyes larger than ever behind the tortoiseshell spectacles.

Max persisted. 'Tell us what you mean. What's coming true?'

The ex-teacher's lip trembled. 'The curse. I thought it was all nonsense, but it isn't. It's catching up with us.'

Libby leaned forward. '*Us?* Who do you mean by *us*?'

The woman's eyes flickered between Libby and Max, seeking sympathy, but Max's face was stony. She wasn't getting away with evasions this time. Her shoulders slumped. 'It's the beads. They're causing it.'

'What rubbish.' Max snorted. 'They're old and possibly valuable, but that's all.'

Libby held out a hand. 'Wait, Max. Let's hear what she has to say.'

The woman's hands trembled, tea spilling on her tweed skirt. 'It's all in the paper.' She took a newspaper from the table. 'Here it is.'

Libby recognised the picture. 'It's that photograph from the excavation, Max. The one you emailed to me.' She took it from Miss Bakewell's shaking fingers and read aloud. *Beads from Glastonbury Lake Village discovered near Deer Leap Stones.*

She frowned. 'I've heard that name, somewhere.'

Miss Bakewell had stopped trembling. The light of an educator shone in her eyes. 'The Deer Leap stones are a pair of ancient standing stones, said to mark the entrance to a tunnel leading to Glastonbury Tor, eight miles away.'

'According to the newspaper,' Libby was scanning the story, 'a man called Roger Johnson was out for a walk last week when he found an amber bead beside the stones. Being a local man, he knew about the archaeological digs and the stories about a tunnel and contacted the newspaper. They're going to have the amber dated.' She looked up from the paper. 'Here's a picture of the bead. What do you think, Max? Is it one of ours?'

Miss Bakewell removed her glasses, breathed on the lenses and scrubbed at them with a scrap of handkerchief. 'A warning,' she whispered. 'That's what it is. From all those years ago.'

Goose-bumps prickled the skin of Libby's arms, but Max snorted. 'Come on. There must be millions of amber beads lying around in jewellery boxes across the country. Amber's not a precious stone and anyone could have dropped it. I bet it's nothing to do with the necklace, anyway,'

Libby cleared her throat. He was right. With any luck, Max hadn't noticed her moment of foolish panic. She said, 'We all know John Williams didn't die because of some magic curse. I heard what you said at the exhibition, Miss Bakewell, when you saw the photographs. It wasn't the beads that bothered you, it was someone you saw in the picture; a friend. You said a name; Catriona. Later, you said, 'It's not her, after all.' What did you mean? Don't you think it's time you told us what happened to this Catriona?'

Miss Bakewell's hand flew to her chest. Colour leached out of her face, leaving her pale, eyes staring. Libby pushed her advantage. 'We're not leaving until you explain.'

The woman seemed to shrink into her chair as she began to talk. 'I knew Catriona well, many years ago, when we were young.

It was a shock, seeing the child in the photograph. She looked so like Catriona. You see, Catriona died.'

Libby gulped. 'How did she die?'

The woman shrugged. 'It was an accident at a party. She fell out of a window. She was on drugs, you see. After all, it was the sixties.'

* * *

Libby and Bear ran after Max as he hurried down the path. The shock of thinking he might be dead had overcome the anger and shame she'd felt when he turned her down. Seeing him safe in Miss Bakewell's house, her heart had leapt. That told Libby everything she needed to know. She was falling for him. Even if Max never returned her feelings, she couldn't bear to lose him from her life. She'd been a fool, doing her best to drive him away, because he'd asked for more time.

She wouldn't make that mistake again. 'Wait for me, Max.'

He turned and smiled, and Libby's heart lurched. It was hard to hide her feelings, now she understood them, but she had to try. 'How much of that did you believe?' There, that sounded sufficiently matter of fact.

'Hardly any. She's trying to pull the wool over our eyes with all that 'curse of the beads' malarkey. Misdirect us.'

Libby nodded. 'I believe Catriona's death is important. When Miss Bakewell saw the girl in the photo and mistook her for the woman who'd died, back in the sixties, she was terrified.'

Libby paused, one hand on the door of the Land Rover. 'It's difficult, sifting through to find out what's true. We don't even know if more beads were really found at Deer Leap. Anyone could tell the press a trumped-up story.'

'Including Miss Bakewell.'

As they fastened their seat belts, Libby pondered. 'No, I don't think she did it. She was genuinely scared.'

'You know what I think?' Max put the key in the ignition. 'I think she's got a thing going for the professor. That's why she's so upset about the explosion. It might have nothing to do with the amber beads.' He turned. 'Libby, are you listening?'

Libby swallowed. 'Sorry.' Her voice shook. She hadn't intended this to happen. She cleared her throat.

'What's the matter?'

If only he'd stop looking at me like that, as if he cares. 'Nothing.'

'Come on. Tell me.'

A sob rose in Libby's throat. She muttered. 'She's not the only one who thought someone died.'

'What?' Two vertical lines appeared between his eyes. 'Oh. You mean...'

Libby sniffed hard, struggling to keep the tears at bay. 'Yes.' She couldn't stop her voice squeaking. 'When I heard about the explosion, I thought you'd been killed.'

'Oh, Libby.' His arms slid round Libby's back, pulling her close. 'I should have realised.'

Her face pressed against his shoulder, his woody scent filling her head. Her voice muffled by his jacket, she muttered, 'The people at the history meeting were ghouls, wondering if anyone died, while all I could think about was – was you.'

Max looked into her eyes. 'I'm so sorry, Libby,' he murmured, and for once there was no hint of sarcasm in his voice or face. 'I didn't think...'

Libby scrubbed her eyes with the back of her hand.

Max smoothed a lock of hair behind her ear. 'I should have realised you'd be upset. I would have been, if it were you.'

'Really?' She tried a laugh. 'I think that's the nicest thing you've ever said.'

'Is it?' The frown was back. 'Then, I should be ashamed of myself. You're a wonderful person, Libby Forest.'

'If that's the beginning of a 'you're too good for me' speech, you can shut up, right now. I'm not a teenager.' The corners of his mouth twitched. 'It's not funny.'

'No.' Max fixed his gaze on the windscreen. The smile had disappeared. 'It's not.' He started the engine. 'I'll drop you off at my place to pick up your car. Miss Bakewell and I called in there to leave it. I couldn't go another mile with my knees wedged against my chin.' He grinned and Libby relaxed. Max was safe and they were friends again. She could take some time to deal with the other problems in her life.

13

TREVOR

That evening, Libby roamed the house, searching for any distraction from the questions hammering in her head. She flicked through every channel on television, dropped the remote control in disgust, and started the latest Diane Saxon novel. She read the first chapter twice. With a groan, she snapped the book shut. She hadn't taken in a single word.

It was Trevor's fault. Libby managed not to think about Jemima Bakewell and the beads, and with a supreme effort of will, she could even force Max Ramshore out of her mind, but she couldn't stop thoughts of Trevor. Every time she remembered her husband and the financial mess he'd left behind, her stomach heaved with anxiety. She'd never rest until she knew the full story of his crimes.

She headed to the study. Fuzzy lay stretched across the computer keyboard, tail dangling in front of the desk drawer. Libby gave her a nudge. 'Shift over, will you?' The cat stared, unmoving, through slitted eyes. Libby pushed harder. 'Come on, you silly animal.'

Fuzzy stretched, sighed, and turned round twice. Libby seized her chance to grab the folder containing Trevor's papers from the drawer, before the cat settled down in exactly the same position as before.

Two cups of coffee later, Libby had read and re-read every word of the documents in the folder; a portfolio of houses, bought with money from criminal activities. All the houses had mortgages due to be paid off in five years' time.

One question kept pounding in her head. Why five years?

She flipped through the documents one final time. For heaven's sake, why hadn't she noticed it before? *Call yourself an investigator?* Libby had spoken aloud. Fuzzy stirred, stretched, and went back to sleep.

The letter about the first mortgage was dated six years ago. Trevor died last year.

She took a shaky breath. Was there the slightest chance Trevor's death had not been from a heart attack?

She shook her head. She was over-dramatising – seeing crime everywhere.

But she'd been involved in two murders since arriving in Exham, even before John Williams died. Both of those had looked, at first glance, like accidents or suicides.

What if Trevor's death was another murder?

* * *

'Mrs F? Shouldn't you be in bed at this time of night?' Libby was making bread, taking out her feelings on the dough.

She registered Mandy's flushed face, smudged lipstick and bright eyes, and thumped the dough harder. 'Looks like you've had fun.'

'What's wrong?' Mandy spooned instant coffee into a mug.

'Won't make you one. You look wired already. You know it's after midnight?'

Libby grunted, pounded the bread into shape, turned it into a tin and dumped it in the oven. 'If that doesn't rise, I'm giving up and moving back to London.'

'Anything I can do?'

Libby swept a cloth over the counter with unnecessary force. 'It's just life.'

'I know. Life sucks.' Mandy rescued a jug of milk. Libby flung the cloth into the sink and flopped onto a stool, head resting on her hands.

'Want to talk?'

'Give me a minute.' It wasn't fair to burden Mandy with her problems. Libby wiped her sleeve across both eyes, blew her nose, and forced a smile on her face. 'Sorry. I was having a moment. About my husband.' Mandy deserved more than that. 'And Max, actually.'

'Men. What are they like?'

Libby managed a watery smile. She wished she could tell Mandy the truth. Her husband was a crook, she suspected he hadn't died of a heart attack after all, and Max had turned down her offer of a relationship. Things couldn't really get worse.

She let her breath out in a long sigh. Mandy had enough problems in her own family. She'd moved in with Libby to escape them and it wasn't fair to dump the landlady's woes on the lodger. 'Cheer me up. Tell me about Steve.'

Mandy's face melted into that dreamy expression only first true love could conjure. The gig had been wonderful, Steve had been amazing, and the audience had been phenomenal. Mandy's enthusiasm, pink cheeks and ear-to-ear grin lifted Libby's mood an inch or two from the mire of gloom. So what if Max didn't share her feelings? Who cared if Trevor hadn't died of natural causes? The world was still turning.

Libby yawned and forced a smile. 'I'm truly happy you had such a good evening. Sorry to be grumpy. Hope I didn't spoil things.'

'You go to bed. I'll take the bread out when it's cooked. Everything will look better in the morning.'

Tears welled in Libby's eyes. Somehow, she and Mandy had reversed their roles. 'I'm sure it will,' she mumbled, like a tired child. Her life was a mess. She didn't want to think about it any more. Far better to keep her mind busy with the murder on the Tor. She thought back to her morning walk on the Tor. Bear had seemed ill, and she'd taken him to Tanya, the vet.

While she was waiting, and the receptionist regaling her with Glastonbury myths, she'd looked at the posters on the walls.

Tanya's framed certificate had been there, in pride of place. Her degree had come from Bristol University, and Libby had smiled. It seemed local people rarely left the South West. Not surprising, really. Apart from the beauty of the region, it boasted one of England's top universities.

Jemima Bakewell had studied there. Libby lay back on the sofa and closed her eyes. If only she could remember the date on Tanya's certificate. Had she, too, been a contemporary of Catriona, and the professor?

14

TANYA

Bear tugged on the lead, dragging Libby through the door of the vet's surgery. Tanya Ross reached for a pack of worming tablets. The dog reared on his hind legs, placed a pair of heavy front paws on her shoulders and licked the vet's face.

Libby tugged his collar. 'Get down, Bear.'

He dropped to all fours as Tanya wiped drool from her cheek. 'I haven't had a hug like that all day.' She eyed Libby. 'There's not much wrong with him today, so how can I help you?'

'I wanted to have a word with you about Jemima Bakewell.'

Tanya's eyes slid away. 'I'm sorry. Who did you say? Bakewell? Like the tarts?' Tension in the vet's voice killed the lame joke.

'I think you know her. Weren't you at University together?' The vet was motionless, as though holding her breath. 'With Jemima Bakewell and Professor Perivale? Bristol in the sixties?'

Libby waved at the certificate on the wall. 'According to that, you were contemporaries.'

Tanya Ross swallowed. 'So what if we were? I haven't seen either of them for years.' She made a show of looking at her watch. 'Now, the receptionist will be back soon, and I've got appointments, so I'll have to ask you to leave.'

'Oh, no. You're not getting rid of me that easily. People have died.'

'Is that any of your business? You don't know them. You've only—'

Libby cut her off with a sigh. 'I know, I've only lived in the area for a short while. If I had a pound for every time one of you locals told me that, I'd be living in one of those houses by the golf course.'

The ghost of a smile spread over Tanya's face. She pushed past Libby. 'Come into my room.' Bear sniffed at Tanya's pockets and the vet brought out a handful of dog treats. She beckoned Libby to follow and opened a door marked *Private*, where racks of professional journals climbed the walls and a computer covered most of the surface of a small desk.

The two women perched on small brown tub chairs, on opposite sides of a cheap, deal coffee table. A textbook lay open on the desk. Libby averted her eyes from a lurid diagram of the lungs and heart of some unknown animal. Tanya snapped the book shut. 'Coffee?'

Libby shook her head. 'Information.'

'I don't see why I should tell you anything.'

'You won't put me off by saying, 'It's none of your business.' I was there, up on the Tor with no one else around except a child, and just after I left, John Williams' body was dumped with a plastic bag round his head. That makes it my business.' Libby remembered every detail. 'That poor child could have found it, and the thought of that makes my blood boil. So, don't tell me to walk away. I'm determined to find out what's been going on. If you know something, you'd better tell me.'

Libby paused, waited and added, 'For Catriona's sake.'

The shot hit home and the vet's mouth dropped open. 'What do you know about Catriona?'

'I know she was your friend. There was a group of you, all at University together. Catriona was one of that group and she died at a party.' The vet shifted, crossing and uncrossing her legs. 'Were you there, the night Catriona died?'

Tanya chewed her lip, her eyes on the table, focused on the closed veterinary textbook. She murmured, 'None of us was in the room when Catriona fell out of the window. We were all downstairs.'

'That's what Miss Bakewell said.' Was that a tiny sigh of relief? Libby let it go, for the moment. If the vet thought she'd side-stepped a difficult question, she'd be likely to open up and tell Libby more than she intended. 'Tell me about Catriona.'

Tanya looked up from the book on the table. Her eyes were very bright. 'She was beautiful. She cared about people. If you had a problem, she'd always listen – really listen.'

Briefly, a smile lit the woman's face, then faded. 'We shared a house, Jemima, Catriona and me, and while we were there, I was happier than I'd ever been in my life. My own home was a place where we kept a stiff upper lip and spoke when we were spoken to. I came to University to escape, and I found Catriona.'

Tanya pressed a balled-up tissue to her eyes. 'I'm sorry. I haven't talked about it for so long.'

Libby, careful not to shatter the woman's mood, kept her voice low. 'You found Catriona and...?'

The vet drew a shaky breath. 'Everything was fine until that night.'

'What night? What happened?'

'It was the May Ball. We were all there. I wore a long, velvet dress. Navy blue. Catriona said it matched my eyes. She had a red top with enormous sleeves. She looked wonderful; like a queen. Even Jemima seemed pretty, that night, but the two of them had far too much to drink and they had a fight over that stupid necklace...' The vet fumbled in her pocket for a new tissue.

'The beads belonged to Jemima, didn't they?'

Tanya's lip curled. 'Malcolm Perivale gave them to her. She said she found them but no one believed her. Malcolm stole the necklace from some dig he was working on in Glastonbury and gave them to her. They were going out together, you see. What he saw in her, no one could understand.'

'What happened to the beads, that night?'

The vet shrugged and stood up. Her voice rang with spite. 'Oh, it was just a storm in a teacup at first but it ended in disaster. Jemima accused Catriona of taking the necklace; as if Catriona would steal things. Or, maybe it was the other way round. It was so long ago; I can't remember exactly. Anyway, they had a quarrel.'

She shrugged. 'It was hot, and the music was loud. Catriona went upstairs to cool down. The next thing we knew, she'd fallen out of the window.'

'She fell? You mean...'

'No one saw her fall.' Tanya's eyes were narrow slits, 'but someone found her on the pavement.'

She shuddered. 'We all ran out to see. There was a huge pool of blood on the paving stones and Catriona was dead. Her skull was crushed by the fall, you see.'

Libby let the vet sit in silence for a moment, reliving that night, before she asked, 'Had Catriona taken LSD?'

Tanya threw her hands in the air. 'Catriona tried everything. She said LSD made her think she'd died and gone to heaven. She saw multi-coloured angels and flowers and heard music. Psychedelic. That's what we called it, in those days.'

'And taking LSD makes people believe they can fly.'

The vet nodded. 'We were such fools.'

15

'Weather doesn't look too good.' Mandy leaned from the kitchen window, eyes on a system of grey clouds scudding across the sky. 'Still, Glastonbury isn't Snowdonia.'

'We won't need climbing boots but we'd better wear water-proofs,' Libby agreed. Mandy was silent, staring at her landlady's hands. She'd taken to watching Libby like an anxious guardian angel since the midnight baking episode. It was touching and infuriating at the same time.

Libby looked down. A dozen expensive chocolate wrappers, bought for the batch of Jumbles chocolates, lay under her fingers, shredded into tiny pieces. She tossed the ruined gold foil in the bin. No need to take her feelings about Trevor out on her work.

The first item on the day's agenda was a visit to the Deer Leap stones. Max decreed it was a wild goose chase. He was probably right, but Libby refused to ignore even the most unlikely clue and he'd agreed to come along.

Bear, at least, was enthusiastic. His head on Mandy's lap, he spent the drive to the Mendip Hills panting, mouth agape. Jumping from the car, he led the way up the path to the stones with tail aloft, sniffing the grass as though on the trail of some truly sensational scent, but when they arrived, he refused to go anywhere near the stones.

Rain clouds hung low, hiding the distant summit of the Tor. Libby pulled her jacket close, shivering from more than the cold. Bear snuffled her leg and she touched him, gently, behind the ears.

'You remember it, too, don't you?' Libby whispered. 'That morning on the Tor. It feels like that, here. I don't like it, either.'

They stood in the field and gazed round, disappointed. 'No sign of a tunnel,' Max pointed out. 'Not that it's at all likely. If it existed, someone would have found it.'

Mandy remained upbeat. 'The Deer Leap stones are here, anyway.' Two upright lumps of rock, set ten yards or so apart, stood alone in the field. 'They're like a piece of Stonehenge.'

'It shows we're in the right place.' Max threw a stick for the dog, but he ignored it, sticking close to Libby.

'Bear doesn't like it here,' Mandy pointed out. 'Maybe there really is a tunnel underground, full of ghosts, and he can sense it.'

'Nonsense.' In an attempt to throw off the gloom that weighed on her shoulders, Libby set off across the field and marched round the boundary, swinging her arms, inspecting the hedges.

Mandy and Max followed her example and spread out, searching every blade of grass.

'We're not going to find anything,' Mandy said at last, 'and I'm getting cold in this wind. Shall we give up?'

Max was on the other side of the field, bending low in a corner, peering at the ground. He beckoned. Suddenly excited, Libby and Mandy ran to join him. 'Have you found something?'

He straightened up, holding out one hand. 'A bead.' It was covered in mud, but Max rubbed away the dirt, uncovering the glow of a reddish-yellow stone.

Mandy breathed, 'It's amber.'

'Now, there's a coincidence.' Max turned the stone in his hand. 'An amber bead, just where we thought it would be.'

Mandy squeaked. 'So, it's all true? There's a tunnel under here? Someone came through from the Tor and dropped the bead and...' She stopped, deflated by her companions' expressions. 'It's all nonsense, isn't it?'

Max grunted. 'Afraid so, Mandy.'

'But look at Bear. Why's he so miserable?'

Max watched the dog. 'Bear relies on his sense of smell. What if he's caught the scent of someone he knows instinctively he can't trust?'

Mandy breathed. 'The murderer?'

Max scratched his chin. 'Someone who left the bead for us to find, is leading us up the garden path, and is probably the killer. The question is, who?'

Libby pulled off her hat and let the wind catch her hair. 'Do you think Miss Bakewell had anything to do with it? I don't trust her.'

Max was nodding. 'I think another interview with our retired schoolteacher is called for, don't you, to find out why she sent us all on this wild goose chase?'

Libby agreed. 'If you ask me, she talks about the amber beads just a little too much, as though she's trying to make us think about them instead of something else. I think she's trying deflection – a sort of sleight of hand. It's making me suspicious.'

'Whatever we decide to do, can we please get away from this place? I'm freezing.' Mandy's face was pinched with cold.

'Let's find a cafe in Glastonbury, get warmed up and have a walk up the Tor,' said Max.

* * *

Half an hour later, stomachs full of scones and jam from a cafe near Glastonbury Abbey, they emerged from the trees at the base of the Tor and trudged up the hill.

'Cheer up,' Mandy said. The cream tea had given her a second wind.

Max walked by Libby, close, but not touching. She kept her gaze averted, like a nervous schoolchild. 'Maybe it's the weather,' she muttered. 'All these dramatic thunder clouds. I think we're in for a soaking.' They were halfway up the hill now and the clouds were gathering fast. 'Do you think we should go back? It's going to rain.'

'Not now,' Mandy pleaded. 'I'm in the mood to see a ghost or two.'

Libby's cry cut her off. 'There she is.' She pointed up the hill where the top of St Michael's Tower disappeared into black clouds.

Max took her arm. 'There's no one there.'

'I saw her.' Libby pulled away. 'Didn't you? She was there – the little girl.' She whirled round. 'And it's no good making faces at Mandy behind my back as if I'm crazy. I saw her, I tell you.'

The first heavy drops of rain began.

'Well,' said Max, 'Whatever you saw, we need to get up to the Tower now, if we're going. We can shelter there. In any case, I don't think we'll make it back down again without getting soaked. In for a penny, in for a pound, as my mother used to say.'

His long legs soon took him ahead. Bear jogged at his side and Mandy did her best to keep up, panting hard. Libby brought up the rear. 'I saw her. I did, and she must be real – if I'd seen a ghost, Bear wouldn't be trotting up so cheerfully. You know he senses things.'

'Hey, I believe you,' Max called back. 'You saw something that wasn't a ghost.'

'I saw the little girl.' They were almost at the top. Rain sliced into Libby's face as she covered the last few yards to the shelter of the Tower. She found Max, Mandy and Bear in the arch at the entrance.

Inside one corner of the Tower, crouched by a stone bench, the child's big eyes stared from a pink raincoat, wet black curls escaping from the furry hood.

'Hello, again,' Libby said. The child stayed still, except for her eyes. They flickered from the adults to the doorway and back. She was poised, ready to run.

Bear trotted over, tongue lolling. The child stretched out a hand and touched his ear. He stood quietly, letting her pet his head.

Libby took a step forward. 'Does your mother know you're here?' The little girl took no notice. Couldn't she talk?

Max murmured in Libby's ear. 'I've got an idea. Let me talk to her.' He pointed to the dog. 'This is Bear. He'd like to know your name.'

The child squatted down, her lips close to Bear's ear and whispered. Libby had to strain to hear.

'Katy,' the child said.

Max went on, 'Bear wants to know if Mummy's here with you, Katy.' The girl stroked Bear's head but said nothing more. 'Or Daddy?'

The child pointed down the hill. The wind had dropped and the rain subsided to a steady drizzle. A figure emerged from the trees. The child waved, and it waved back.

'Shall we go and talk to him? Bear will come too.'

She nodded.

The man that met the little procession halfway up the hill looked about forty, despite the long blonde dreadlocks tied at the back of his head. A hole in one elbow and a couple of missing buttons spoiled what must once have been a good leather jacket. 'Af'ernoon,' he nodded.

Max said, 'Is this your daughter? Shouldn't she be at school?'

The man ignored the question. 'Talked to you, did she?'

Libby said, 'Not us. To Bear – the dog.'

'Ah. She'll talk to animals, will Katy. Not to people, though.'

'Why not?'

He pulled at his goatee beard as though deciding whether to answer. 'She don't like people much.'

'Fair enough.' Max nodded and walked on, a hand on Libby's elbow.

'Why did you drag me away? We should have asked a few more questions,' she hissed as soon as they were out of earshot.

'None of our business, is it? Katy's with her father. She's perfectly safe.'

'I wonder why she won't talk. Do you think there's something wrong with her?'

Max shook his head. 'Some children can't bring themselves to talk out loud. Especially to grownups; they feel overwhelmed. Animals are less demanding or scary.'

Libby thought back to her first meeting with the little girl. 'I wonder where her father was last time I saw her. Down in the mist, I suppose. I let my imagination run away with me that day. I was almost ready to believe in fairies.'

'Wait.' The man called. 'Aren't you that detective woman. The one that was in the papers when the singer died?'

Max murmured, 'You're famous.'

Libby ignored him. 'Yes, that's me? Why?'

'Maybe you can help us. We've lost something, you see. Something that matters to Katy. We need to find it.'

'Is that why Katy's on the Tor?'

He nodded. 'She runs away, that's the trouble. Any chance she gets, she runs up here, looking for it.'

Libby had a moment of inspiration. 'The necklace?'

The man laughed. 'Fancy you knowing that. She's attached to those old beads. Been in the family for forty years or more.'

Libby, spirits rising, reached into her bag and fumbled with the zip. 'Here it is.'

She held up the necklace. She'd polished the beads until they gleamed and threaded them on a length of stout leather. 'The wire was broken. I expect that's how she lost them.'

Katy's father took the beads, running them through his fingers. 'Katy,' he shouted. 'Get over 'ere.'

The child saw the beads and held out a grubby hand. Her father dropped the necklace on her palm. A grin spread over the child's face, colour flooded her cheeks and she looked, suddenly, just like any other happy little girl.

'Thank the nice lady,' said her father.

The child's smile died. She inspected her feet.

'Actually,' Libby said, 'it's Bear you have to thank. If it hadn't been for him, I wouldn't have found the beads.'

Katy sank on to her knees and threw her arms round the dog's neck.

'Thank you, Bear,' she whispered.

16

TRUFFLES

'You've got some explaining to do.' Libby had hammered on Jemima Bakewell's door until the woman came running. Libby's face burned with fury. 'All that nonsense about beads and legends.'

Jemima Bakewell held the door ajar. 'I suppose you'd better come in.'

'It's about time you started telling the truth.' Libby refused to sit, choosing instead to stand by the window, so she could see every twitch of Miss Bakewell's face. 'Who is Katy, how do you know her, why does she have your beads, and why didn't you tell me the truth from the beginning?'

Miss Bakewell perched on the edge of the sofa. 'What do you know about Katy?'

'We went up the Tor and she was there again, looking for the beads. We met her father.'

Miss Bakewell snorted. 'He's a useless article, that man. Always been a cup short of a tea service. Even at school.' She rolled her eyes. 'I taught him once. Nothing stayed in that head. Had to be kind to him, though, given...' she stopped.

'It's no good, Miss Bakewell.' Libby was stern. 'You won't get away with half answers, not this time. Nor talking about ancient history or myths and legends. I need the truth.'

'No.' The woman suddenly stopped twisting her hands. She folded her arms. 'What's past is past.'

'But John Williams died,' Libby shouted. 'Have you forgotten? Don't you care?'

Miss Bakewell's face crumpled. 'Of course, I care, but there's nothing more I can do.'

'You can tell us the truth.'

The woman strode across the room and threw the door open. 'I can't tell you anything. Now, please leave my house and don't come back.'

* * *

Libby met Max on the beach. He'd phoned, sounding uncertain, to suggest they walk the dogs together. 'Are we still partners?'

'Of course, we are, but we're no farther forward.' She tried to sound neutral. 'Miss Bakewell called my bluff, just when I thought she was about to tell me everything.'

Max was thoughtful. 'She knows who killed John Williams and she knows why.' He walked faster. 'Come on. I think best when I'm moving. Let's find some sticks for the dogs.'

The sun was back, there were no signs of yesterday's rain clouds, and the beach was thronged with visitors enjoying the heat.

Libby pulled off her jacket and a sweater as her spirits rose. 'This is proper summer weather.'

'Now, let's have a look at the facts,' Max suggested. 'Come on, Libby, this is what you do best. Sort out the truth from all this misdirection.'

'Misdirection.' Yes, that was the problem. Someone had been orchestrating events to throw Libby off the scent. 'It's like a magic show,' Libby said, trying to untangle her thoughts. 'We need to keep the facts separate from the special effects.'

She used Shipley's stick to write numbers in the sand. 'Number one fact; the death of John Williams on the Tor. That really happened. That day was a muddle because after I was caught in the mist, I met Katy on her own, then found the beads. Bear was chilled and unhappy, and I panicked, thinking he was ill. I can see things more clearly, now. The beads are 2,000 years old, but the myths around them are just stories. The beads belonged to Katy – or, at least, she had them in her possession.'

Max put in, 'How did she come by them in the first place?'

'Her father said they'd been in the family a long time. Forty years. Miss Bakewell had them first.'

'Right, that's one question we'll have to answer. How did the beads get from our teacher to Katy? We'll need to find that out. But, going back to the facts...'

Max drew the number two, then threw the stick for Shipley to chase. 'Miss Bakewell, Tanya Ross and the professor all admit they knew each other, plus Catriona and John Williams.'

Libby nodded. She looked around for another stick but found nothing. She used a finger to draw in the sand, instead. 'Fact number three. The body was found on the Tor, the day before the exhibition. John Williams was killed because someone wanted to stop the exhibition.'

Max nodded. 'That didn't work, and Miss Bakewell stole the photos. Fact number four.'

'Don't forget number five, the explosion on the day Miss Bakewell went to see the professor. That's another coincidence. A lot of them about, aren't there?'

They looked at each other. Libby was the first to speak again.

'Things don't look too good for Jemima Bakewell. She's involved in everything. No wonder she won't talk to me any more.'

'But we still don't understand what else links all our facts together. If Miss Bakewell's been going around killing people, there must be some sort of a reason.'

'Unless she's just a nut case.'

* * *

The doorbell rang. 'Mandy, can you get it?' Libby called, forgetting Mandy was out. She cursed, shouted, 'Just a minute,' and elbowed the tap. Tempering chocolate helped her think, but it was a messy business. She was still drying her hands as she opened the door. 'Miss Bakewell?'

'Can I come in?'

'I suppose so.' When would Libby remember to use the safety chain? She ushered the teacher to the sitting room, wondering how to tell if her visitor had any sort of a weapon in that familiar brown handbag.

'How did you get my address?'

'Oh, dear me, you're quite famous, Mrs Forest. Everyone knows you live at Hope Cottage. It was in the paper when you solved the murder on the beach.'

Libby swallowed. She didn't like that idea at all.

Fuzzy, stretched on the sofa, opened one eye but to Libby's surprise, she stayed where she was.

'What a lovely animal.' Miss Bakewell held out a hand. Fuzzy sniffed at the fingers and allowed the newcomer to stroke her cheek. 'I've always had cats, you know, until a few months ago when poor Sebastian had to be put down.'

Fuzzy seemed to trust the woman. Weren't cats supposed to have a sixth sense? Maybe Fuzzy lost hers by spending too much time asleep in the airing cupboard. Libby felt torn between sympathy for this lonely woman and frustration with all her stories. 'Do you eat chocolate?'

Her visitor beamed.

Libby piled a tray with coffee, cream, and a plate of chocolate mis-shapes from the kitchen, seizing the opportunity to send a text to Max.

Get here now. Miss B's here – I think she's about to confess.

No need to tell Max about the hairs standing on the back of Libby's neck, like a warning not to trust anyone.

Cheeks pink with delight, Miss Bakewell considered, fingers hovering over odd shaped coffee creams and squashed strawberry shortcakes before settling on a wonky white chocolate truffle. 'You sell these in the bakery in Exham, don't you? I bought a box recently. For a friend, of course.'

She wagged a finger. 'Now, just a word of warning. Don't let that dog of yours anywhere near chocolate. It's poison to dogs, you know.'

'I did know, actually.' Had the woman come to confess or give unwanted advice?

Libby cut to the chase. 'I hope you're here to tell me what's been going on.'

Miss Bakewell, taken by surprise, swallowed the last of the truffle with an audible gulp. 'Oh.' She recovered. 'Very well. I think you and your friend, Mr Ramshore, may have jumped to the wrong conclusions.'

'Do you?' Libby kept her voice non-committal.

'Yes, you see, when you asked me about little Katy, I didn't tell you everything.'

'As far as I remember, you didn't tell us anything useful.'

'You and that friend of yours – Max, isn't it – were very kind, after that dreadful explosion, so I decided you should know the truth.'

Libby held out the plate and Miss Bakewell selected another chocolate.

'Let me guess,' Libby prompted. 'We know you were one of the group of friends at University with John Williams and Professor Perivale. You visited the professor even though you'd kept away from each other for so many years. You wanted to know if he had the beads, didn't you? You're obsessed by them. Did you cause the explosion?'

Miss Bakewell sat ramrod straight. Two pink spots appeared on her cheeks. 'No, no, you've got it all wrong. I wouldn't do a thing like that. I'll be frank. I went to see Malcolm, as you say, to beg for the beads. You see, nothing's been right in my life since I lost them. Nothing.'

The pink flush deepened to purple. The teacher's lips suddenly curled. 'They were mine.'

The doorbell rang. Miss Bakewell clamped her lips together and Libby winced.

Max's eyes sparkled. 'Am I in time?'

'Your timing couldn't be worse,' Libby hissed as she let him in. 'She was just about to spill the beans. Don't upset her.'

She returned to Miss Bakewell and offered an encouraging smile. 'You can tell Mr Ramshore the truth. We're partners.'

The teacher looked at Max as though he were an insect in a bowl of cereal. 'Very well, if you insist. Where was I?'

'Let's go back a bit. Explain what happened at University.'

'There were several of us. All friends together. It was the sixties – well before your time. I'm afraid we experimented with some rather inappropriate substances.'

Max chuckled. 'The generation that invented sex.'

Libby glared, but the teacher ignored him. 'There were five of us in all.'

Libby counted them off. 'You and the professor, John Williams and Catriona. That's four, plus Tanya, the vet.'

'Catriona,' said Max. 'You recognised them in the photograph you stole.'

Miss Bakewell's lips trembled. 'I thought it would all come out if people saw the pictures. It was so long ago. When I read about the exhibition in the local news, I couldn't sleep. How could John show everyone? Why couldn't he leave well alone?'

'Show everyone what?'

'The pictures of us all – of Catriona.'

Libby nodded. 'It was all about Catriona, wasn't it?'

Miss Bakewell paused, blinking. 'I wonder if I could perhaps have another chocolate. And a glass of water?'

Libby fought an urge to grab the woman by the throat and shake her. She raised a hand, warning Max not to interrupt, fetched water and offered more chocolates. Miss Bakewell sucked a salted caramel, making it last, as Libby forced herself to count to a hundred.

She reached ninety and the wait was finally over. 'John put photographs of Catriona in the exhibition, and I had to hide them. I couldn't let anyone recognise her because – because she looked exactly like that child.'

'Katy,' said Libby. She smiled, realising her intuition had been correct. 'I think Catriona was Katy's grandmother.'

Miss Bakewell heaved a sigh. 'The likeness is unmistakable.'

Max said. 'Which of you killed Catriona?'

Miss Bakewell gasped. 'I – we didn't. She fell – it was an accident – we were at a party. I told you, it was the sixties. She'd taken something – LSD, I suppose. She went upstairs to find her coat and she fell.'

Libby leaned forward, trying to read the teacher's face. 'That's not the whole truth, is it? What really happened?'

Miss Bakewell's lip curled. 'You have to understand. Catriona was always wild. She looked lovely, of course. Her face was quite exquisite, so of course everyone adored her.' The words dripped with sarcasm. 'When Catriona was around, the rest of us faded into the background. She outshone us all in every way, and what's more, she knew it and used it.'

She glared. 'Catriona was a mean, spiteful cat. She won her place at University by flirting in the interview; the interviewers were all men, of course. She wanted to be an architect, like her father. He died when she was very young. She shouldn't have been at a University like Bristol. She couldn't cope with the work and she was jealous of those of us who could. There was nothing Catriona liked more than spoiling things for the rest of us – especially me. Of course, all the men worshipped her.'

'Including the professor?'

'He wasn't a professor then. I met him first, before Catriona, and we were a couple. I thought we'd get married, and...' She took a bite from a chocolate, swallowing hard. 'Catriona set out to take Malcolm away from me. She was always there, in between him and me, looking pretty and fluttering those long eyelashes.

'Of course, she succeeded. She stole my fiancé from me.' She took a long, shuddering breath. 'Men are so superficial.' She spat out the last words, with a venomous look at Max.

Max started, as though about to speak, but changed his mind and let Miss Bakewell continue. 'When she managed to get her hooks into Malcolm, Catriona set her sights on my beads. She had to have them, just because I loved them.'

She banged her fist on the arm of the chair. 'They were all I had left of – of Malcolm and me. He'd taken them from the dig, just for me, but Catriona persuaded him to give them to her. He threatened to tell the University authorities I'd stolen the beads if I didn't hand them over.'

Tears tracked down Miss Bakewell's cheeks. She whispered, 'How could he be so cruel? I did nothing wrong. It was Catriona's fault. She made him hate me.'

Max leaned back; eyes half closed. 'You must realise you've given yourself the perfect motive for killing Catriona.'

17

CHOCOLATE AND WHISKY

It took liberal doses of chocolate and whisky to calm Miss Bakewell. At last she departed, leaving Libby and Max confused. 'It's no good,' Libby yawned. 'My head's spinning and I can't think any more today.'

'No,' Max said. 'You're right. We'll talk again tomorrow.'

Libby spent an hour in the kitchen, piping flourishes on chocolates destined for Jumbles, pleased to finish the batch. The chocolate turned her stomach a little. It reminded her too vividly of Miss Bakewell, filling her face with sweets as she vented her hatred of Catriona. Her feelings had run deep. It was perfectly possible that in a burst of fury, she'd killed Catriona. If the evening had been hot, like today, Catriona may have stood by the open window or even perched on the windowsill. A single push could have tipped her out.

John Williams was another matter. Miss Bakewell was nowhere near strong enough to force a plastic bag over a grown man's head or carry his dead weight up the hill. Perhaps Libby was wrong and the man really had killed himself; the police investigation appeared to have gone quiet. If you were going to end it all, the summit of Glastonbury Tor was as suitable a place as any.

Libby cleaned the kitchen until every inch sparkled. She was too tired to bake, although she had to finish the Jumbles order soon. She needed a bath, to wash away the smell of chocolate. She'd lie in warm bubbles, let her mind wander, and hope her subconscious would sort out the interlocking strands of recent events.

Upstairs, the airing cupboard door was ajar as usual. Fuzzy liked to lie, full stretch, on the best towels, shedding orange fur that resisted every attempt at removal, but she wasn't there now. Libby called her name, but nothing happened. No surprise there. Fuzzy never came when she was called.

Libby dropped the plug in the bath and turned on the taps, at full tilt, squeezing in half a bottle of ridiculously expensive bubble lotion. The water level rose, and she prepared to step in, trying to ignore the faint anxiety tugging at her. When did she last see Fuzzy?

It was no use. She turned off the tap, slid a dressing gown round her shoulders and perched on the edge of the bathtub, thinking. After Miss Bakewell left, the cat refused to eat the bowl of cat food Libby offered; had sashayed, tail aloft, through the cat flap and disappeared. Libby hadn't seen her since.

Fuzzy liked to stretch out on top of the computer in the study. Libby looked there, found no sign of her and moved on to the bedroom. Fuzzy was nowhere to be seen. Libby ran downstairs, half expecting Fuzzy to trip her up. She searched the house from top to bottom, even upending the kitchen bin in case Fuzzy had taken it into her head to sleep in there. The creature had chosen far worse places in the past but wasn't there today. Maybe the garage?

On hands and knees, Libby crawled around the Citroen,

peering under the body at the mysterious underside. What on earth were all those pipes for? She searched every inch of the garage, poking in empty cardboard boxes, peeking inside a roll of carpet and opening the doors of an old cupboard left over from the kitchen renovation.

When there was nowhere else to search, she returned to the house, grabbed a box of dry cat food and walked round the garden, shaking the box and calling. It was crazy to feel so anxious. Cats look after themselves. Everyone knows that, and Fuzzy was more independent than most. It was just nerves, that was the problem. Libby wished Mandy were here. There was no one more down to earth than her Goth lodger.

The sun remained high in the sky throughout the evening, for midsummer was only a few days away. The house was hot, and stuffy. Maybe she should stop worrying about the cat and take that bath, after all.

The water steamed gently, cooling in the tub. Libby turned to close the door and hesitated. Suddenly nervous, she didn't want to be alone and cut off behind a locked door, but she certainly wasn't about to take a bath with the door unlatched. She leaned over, grabbed the plug and, as the water drained away, stepped in and took a quick shower. The noise of the water drowned out all noise. She wouldn't hear Fuzzy.

She grabbed a towel, rubbed until she was dry, and dressed in jeans and a jumper. She wouldn't relax until that cat came home. 'Fuzzy. Fuzzy, where are you? Come on, you stupid cat. Stop playing games.'

Was Libby going to have to make some of those 'Have you seen my cat?' notices to fix to the lampposts? She was fast turning into an old cat lady.

* * *

Libby slipped on a pair of wellies. She'd take a final look through the nearby lanes, before she gave up. She left the rows of houses behind, turning across a main road to a tree lined footpath that led onto the water meadows. *When I get my hands on that cat...*

'Meow.' The noise came from deep inside a hedgerow.

Libby swept aside layers of foliage and found a marmalade tail. She knelt down, following the tail along the fluffy, bedraggled body, to Fuzzy's head. 'Hey, there,' she whispered.

Fuzzy meowed again, the noise pitiful.

'What's happened to you?' One of Fuzzy's hind legs stuck out at an angle. 'Was it a dog?' Fuzzy had a habit of teasing dogs, staying just out of their reach, driving the animals wild. This time she might have got too close, or met a fitter, cleverer animal.

Libby slipped off her light summer jacket and eased it around the cat's body. Fuzzy purred. 'That's right. I'm trying to help.'

She carried the cat, wrapped in her coat, back to the cottage and rang the vet's number, expecting to hear a recorded message. Instead, Tanya Ross answered, voice muffled as though eating. Libby shot a glance at her watch. It was definitely out of office hours.

'I'm so sorry to bother you,' she began, and heard a sigh on the other end, 'But my cat's had an accident. I think she's broken her leg.'

The vet paused, probably swallowing a mouthful of dinner. 'Where are you?' Libby gave her address. 'Oh, you're so near. I'm not really open in the evenings but I don't mind, just this once. Come around here.'

The cat's wicker carrier lived in the boot of Libby's faithful purple Citroen. She eased Fuzzy inside and fitted it into the front passenger seat, securing it with the seatbelt. Fuzzy seemed very tiny, huddled against the side of the basket.

Libby begged the car, 'Please start.' It was becoming more and more eccentric with every passing month, but today, the Citroen was on its best behaviour. Sliding into gear with unusual care, Libby drove to the vet's practice in town. 'This is so kind,' she murmured. 'I know it's late.'

'No trouble.'

Libby forced a smile. 'Is it serious?'

The vet was gentle with Fuzzy, stroking the cat's head as she examined the leg. 'You'll have to leave her with me. It looks like a fracture and if I'm right, she'll need surgery. I'll have to give her a general anaesthetic.'

Fuzzy's eyes were huge, her gaze soulful. 'Whatever she needs.'

At least Tanya Ross sounded hopeful. Libby's heart rate settled.

'How did it happen?'

'I don't really know. She might have been run over, I suppose, though she's a pretty wily animal. She usually keeps well out of the way of traffic. We lived in London for years.'

Tanya's head came up, her eyes boring into Libby's. 'You've had a spell of bad luck. Your dog was ill, up on the hill, then you fell over the cliff, and now this. Maybe you should take a little more care.'

Libby swallowed, the prickles of fear she'd felt that first morning on the Tor, returning. 'How did you know about my fall?'

'News gets around.' The vet's eyes gleamed, pale in the bright overhead strip lights of the surgery. Libby concentrated on keeping her breath slow and steady.

The vet went on, 'I hear you've met that funny little girl that runs around on the Tor. She should be in school. I don't know what her father's thinking.'

'She's very odd. She wouldn't talk to me. All she would do was whisper to the dog.'

Tanya's head shot up. 'She spoke to him. Really? Does her father know?'

'He said it's only people that frighten her. Why? Is there something wrong?'

The vet looked down. 'She's a strange little thing. Born too close to the Tor, that's the story, one midsummer night. Folk see lights dancing around the summit at that time of year, you know.'

Libby groaned. 'Look, I've had enough of local ghost stories. Mysterious lights. Beads that bring bad luck. It's a load of nonsense that you and Miss Bakewell use to throw me off the scent whenever I get close to the truth.'

Colour had drained from the vet's face.

Libby was right, then. 'Miss Bakewell told me about Catriona's death.'

As Tanya Ross gaped, Libby went on, 'You were one of that little group of friends and rivals, all at University together, as I suspected. John Williams used to take photographs of you all and his exhibition brought those days back.

'You must have been horrified when you heard about his retrospective exhibition. Miss Bakewell went along and her fears were confirmed. She took some of the photographs, to keep them secret. For a while, I misunderstood. I thought her concerns were around the necklace – who it belonged to, and where it was found. I was wrong. It wasn't seeing the necklace that gave her such a fright. It was the likeness between Catriona and little Katy.'

She paused, watching Tanya closely. 'The link between Catriona and Katy is at the bottom of all this. Come now, Tanya. Things are serious. John Williams is dead and the professor was nearly killed in an explosion. I think you know what's going on.'

The vet licked her lips and swallowed. Her eyes were on the door, as if she hoped someone would interrupt, but Libby wasn't going to stop. 'Jemima Bakewell hated Catriona, but you didn't. You loved her and you were jealous because she was with Malcolm Perivale. Did you quarrel with her that night because you couldn't have her for yourself?'

Tanya Ross filled a syringe from a bottle. When she turned back, her colour was high and her chin thrust out, as though she'd made up her mind. 'Hold your cat steady,' she commanded. 'I'll tell you the story – at least, the parts I know.'

She slipped the needle into the fur around Fuzzy's neck, but the cat hardly stirred. 'Much of what you say is right; I did love Catriona but I knew she didn't really care for me. Even I could see she was spoiled – too attractive for her own good, but envious of other people's happiness. I wasn't surprised when she set her heart on Malcolm. He was with Jemima and so Catriona wanted him. She liked everything to turn out the way she planned.'

The vet gave a little, sad laugh. 'She wanted to be an architect and she managed to talk her way into a place at one of the best universities in the country. She wanted Malcolm Perivale and it was the easiest thing in the world for her to take him from Jemima. She should have been happy, but...'

She looked straight at Libby. 'She had a secret. She told me about it. She trusted me, because she knew how I felt about her, even though she didn't return my feelings.'

The sadness in Tanya's face reminded Libby of Jemima. 'Catriona needed men like she needed air to breathe. She couldn't help herself – she fell in love with one man after another. She could tell me, because I was no threat. I never cared for men. She felt safe, confiding in me, and she told me about all her conquests. I begged her to be careful, but she wouldn't listen. The university doctor prescribed the contraceptive pill for her, but she often forgot to take it.'

Tanya stroked Fluffy. The cat's eyes closed, her breathing getting deeper. 'Catriona used to say, 'It'll be fine, don't fuss,' but of course, the inevitable happened. She fell pregnant and she was distraught. She could hardly believe such a thing would happen to her. She imagined all her dreams of a future career disappearing if she left university to bring up the baby.'

Tanya avoided Libby's eyes. 'She gave him up for adoption. She couldn't bear to let anything stand in the way of her future.'

'Not even her own child?' Try as she might, Libby found it impossible to hide her shock.

Tanya's eyes met Libby's, hard and bright with unshed tears. 'Don't you dare judge her. Things were different, in those days. It broke Catriona's heart to give away her son.'

The vet gulped and dashed a hand over her eyes. 'When she fell from the window that night, she dropped the necklace – the amber beads she'd fought Jemima to keep. I ran outside when we heard the noise of her fall – that dreadful sound. I saw the necklace on the pavement, by her head, and I picked it up. No one noticed, they were all too busy watching Catriona's blood seep all over the pavement.'

She blew her nose. 'The necklace was her only legacy to her child. I would have liked to keep it, but I knew her son should have it, so I passed it to the couple who adopted Sam. I knew that's what Catriona would have wanted. Sam's new parents kept it for him and he passed it on to his daughter, Katy.'

So, that was how the little girl came by the beads. 'Did Jemima Bakewell know about the pregnancy?'

The vet shrugged. 'I don't know; we never mentioned it, and Catriona disappeared for six months to have the baby. The story was, she was working for an architect – some of the courses included practical placements, so the other students believed her. She thought everything would be all right. There was no need for her to die.'

'No need...' Libby stopped in mid-sentence. Slowly, the pieces of the jigsaw fell into place in her mind. 'I can think of a very good reason why someone thought Catriona needed to die. And there's someone else in danger, right now.'

18

Max's Jaguar squealed to a halt outside the vet's surgery. Libby jumped inside, pulling on her jacket. Adrenalin pumped through her body.

Max's hands were light on the wheel. 'Good of you to call. Mind telling me why you need to get to Miss Bakewell in such a hurry? I left Bear behind – he wasn't happy with me. He thinks he's missing a treat.'

Libby was silent, leaning forward, straining to see the lanes in the dark. 'Can't you go any faster?'

'We're there.' She was out of the car and running up the path before Max had pulled on the handbrake.

He shouted, 'Come back, you idiot.'

She pounded the door with her right hand, left thumb hard on the bell, but no one came. She jabbed the letter box open, shouting. 'Jemima. Miss Bakewell. Let me in.'

Slowly, the door inched open, jamming on the chain. The ex-schoolteacher's eyes peered round the door. Her mouth trembled. 'You can't come in.'

'Open the door, Jemima.' The teacher shook her head. 'You can't...' she whispered. 'I'm busy.'

Libby raised her voice. 'The police are on their way. They'll be here in a moment.'

The door slammed shut. Max said, 'Stay here.'

To a backdrop of wailing sirens and flashing lights, he took off at a run, trampled over flowerbeds, cursing as he crashed into a rubbish bin. He leapt over a side gate and disappeared around the back of the house.

'Stay where you are, Mrs F.' Joe Ramshore jumped from the first police car as it squealed to a halt, lights flashing, and followed his father. A young detective constable circled round the other side of the house.

With a rattle, the front door flew open. Libby pushed past a terrified Jemima Bakewell and ran through the building, emerging at the back, just in time to see Max in the garden, rolling on the grass. His opponent was aiming ineffectual punches at his face as Joe arrived and, in seconds, the man was in handcuffs.

Max brushed mud from his trousers. 'Well, Professor, don't you think it's time to give in? You're really too old for this sort of thing.'

* * *

Mandy will be furious to have missed the fun. She'd been putting in extra hours at the bakery, saving for a holiday in Cornwall with Steve before he left for college.

Libby made tea, once more adding a dash of whisky to Miss Bakewell's cup. After a moment's thought, she added a bigger dash to her own.

Miss Bakewell fussed in cupboards, looking for chocolate

hobnobs, as though Libby and Max were ordinary visitors invited into her home for a chat.

Max was stern. 'Time to explain yourself, Miss Bakewell. And let's drop all the ancient 'curse of the beads' flim-flam.'

Libby giggled, elation making her foolish. *Flim-flam?*

Max shot her a warning glance and she subsided onto a chair. 'Yes, you'd better come clean. We know what's been going on.'

Miss Bakewell picked at a thread hanging from her tweed skirt. 'I suppose the story has to come out now.' The woman's self-possession was astonishing. The professor had been close behind as she opened the door, a kitchen knife in his hand. She'd been in terrible danger, yet she was quite calm.

Libby shuddered to think what might have happened if she and Max hadn't arrived. 'Is there anyone who'll come and look after you?'

Miss Bakewell shrugged. 'I'm used to being alone.'

'You've been in love with the professor all these years, haven't you?'

The elderly spinster let out a long sigh. 'We had so much in common, Malcolm and I. I knew him first, at university. My mistake was introducing him to Catriona. He fell in love with her and made me give the necklace back to him. She wanted it so badly, you see. Malcolm said he'd tell the authorities I stole the beads if I didn't hand them back.'

The man was a monster. 'What really happened at the party? We've heard so many different versions.'

'It was the sixties, so there was drink everywhere, and drugs. Catriona was drunk and high, and Malcolm danced with me.' Her face lit up at the memory, then her lips quivered, 'I was so happy, thinking he'd come back to me, but later I realised he only did it to make Catriona jealous.'

She gulped her tea and held out the cup. 'I think I need a refill.'

As Libby obliged, she went on, 'I'm afraid the details are a bit blurry. I'd had too much to drink, and the Professor and I...' An ugly blush disfigured the teacher's face. 'He took me upstairs to – you know.'

Libby smiled sympathetically as the blush deepened. 'Anyway, Catriona burst in, screeching like a crazy woman. They had a fight, right there in the bedroom, and Catriona screamed at Malcolm, saying it was his fault she'd had to give away her baby and she'd tell everyone he was the father.'

A sudden flash of spite lit Miss Bakewell's face. 'You can imagine what that did to the professor. He was on the way to a great career at the university. He'd be ruined if people found out. He lost his temper and ran at her. She backed away, against the window. It was open. You see, I told you, she fell out of the window.'

Max broke in, 'But she didn't fall, did she? The professor pushed her.'

Miss Bakewell's hands fluttered round her neck, as though feeling the invisible beads. 'I never knew, not for sure. Our little group stuck together after it happened. Malcolm was the cleverest of us all. He was going to do great things and we were his friends. He couldn't have the truth about Catriona's baby getting out. It would ruin any chance of employment at the university, back in those days. He insisted Catriona's fall was an accident.'

Libby said, 'But you all knew. I think you're still lying to us. You guessed the truth about Catriona's absence that summer, you found out about the baby, and you told Malcolm Perivale. You thought he'd break up with her and come back to you, but you were wrong. You underestimated the cold-blooded ambition of the man. He wouldn't let anything get in the way of his career, and he couldn't trust Catriona to keep the baby quiet. Who knows, she might even have talked about getting her child back. He couldn't take the chance. We'll never know whether he pushed Catriona to her death, or she lost her balance and fell, but either way, it let him off the hook.' Libby shuddered. 'With Catriona out of the way and the child safely adopted, the professor got away without a stain on his character.'

'We made a pact not to meet again, but I couldn't forget him. I put him on a pedestal. In my eyes, no one could measure up to him.' Miss Bakewell sounded desolate. 'I wasted my life dreaming of someone who never existed.' She sighed. 'At least I can see the truth now.'

Libby's heart went out to her, but she had one more question. 'Did you plant the single amber bead in the field?'

'I'm afraid I did. I thought another strand to the myths about Glastonbury Tor would muddy the waters enough to make you forget about the professor.'

Max folded his arms. 'He deserves to pay for what he did, although I'm not sure the police have enough evidence to convict him of John William's murder. At the moment, they're questioning him about the explosion. But why did he start killing people now, after so many years?'

Libby said, 'It was the photographic exhibition. The professor killed John to stop it, afraid there would be photos of Catriona. He didn't want people to remember Catriona's death, or discover she had his child. Deluded, pompous man, all he cared about was his reputation.'

Miss Bakewell's head wagged. 'That's right. I suppose he lured John up to the top of the Tor with some story about the old days. He's strong, the professor, and John was so small and slight. All Malcolm had to do was trip John up, get the plastic bag over his head and sit on him until he died. But then the exhibition went ahead, anyway. That Chesterton Wendlebury wouldn't waste the money his company spent on setting it up. He said it was a tribute to John.' Her eyes flashed. 'I went to see the photographs, not even thinking about Catriona, but when I saw that familiar face, I panicked. There she was – Catriona. Except, as you discovered, it wasn't Catriona at all, but her granddaughter. The photograph brought those days back to me, and I think I went a little crazy.'

Libby said, 'Why wouldn't you open the door to me?'

Miss Bakewell took a bite from the last biscuit. 'Malcolm was inside my house. I'd let him in, thinking he was coming back to me at last, but instead, he threatened me. When you knocked on the door, he stood behind me, hissing in my ear that he'd kill you if you came inside. He was so angry, I was terrified.'

Libby said, 'You put yourself in danger to stop him hurting me?' Who'd have thought Miss Bakewell had such courage.

'I'm getting on – it doesn't matter what happens to me, but you're still young.'

Libby frowned. 'I don't know how I can thank you.'

'Why, Mr Ramshore's already returned the favour. Let's call it even.' Miss Bakewell smiled, a genuine, wide smile. 'And perhaps you could invite me along to the Exham History Society one day, to talk about the ancient history of Somerset. It would give me such pleasure – I've missed teaching, so very much.'

* * *

Back in the car, Libby shivered. 'She's a little odd, but very brave. She probably saved my life.'

'The professor was cleaning up his mess and she was next on the list.'

'Poor soul. Keeping the flame of love alive for so long, and for a ruthless killer like the professor. We should keep in touch with her. She seems so lonely.'

Libby thought about the child; the grandchild of foolish, selfish Catriona and the cold, calculating professor. What an ancestry. 'Do you think Katy will ever talk properly?'

Max grinned, a little sheepishly. 'I told her father I'd take Bear over to see her, now and then. Well, quite often, really. Sam reckons she's already taken the first steps to recovery from whatever they call it – elective mutism, I believe. And if she's got the beads, she won't keep running away to look for them on the Tor.'

'The Tor. All that nonsense about the beads bringing bad luck. It's just another story to add to all the others.' Libby laughed. 'Funny, how easy it is to start believing in the supernatural, when all the time there was an explanation for everything that happened.'

Max drew to a halt. 'Libby,' he said. 'I know you're angry with me about Trevor. I'm sorry I didn't tell you everything. I wanted to be sure.' His arm slid round her shoulders. 'I should have trusted you.'

'Yes, you should.' Libby longed to lean her head on his shoulder. His arm was so comforting. She took a long breath. 'I think I can forgive you, Max, but not quite yet. You see, I trusted Trevor for all those years, but he was making a fool of me. I have to sort things out in my own mind. Did he love me? Was he a wicked man, or just a silly, weak one who controlled me because he couldn't control himself? I can't decide, and it's driving me mad. I need the full story.'

19

SHARK

The sun was already beating down on Exham when Libby woke two days later; perfect weather for a run on the beach with Shipley.

First, she checked on Fuzzy. She'd returned from the vet wearing a heavy plaster on her leg, but otherwise back to normal. Scorning the padded basket and blanket Libby had set up, she'd spent most of yesterday sleeping along the back of the sofa, descending only to nibble special treats from the dish Libby had situated close by, and to use the carefully positioned litter tray.

Pleased to see Fuzzy almost back to normal, Libby thought it safe to leave her and take Shipley for a run on the beach.

She heard his frenzied bark as she approached the house. Marina took longer than usual to open the door, and at first sight, looked flustered. Her hair stuck out at wild angles and the top of her frilly blouse drooped, unfastened.

'You'd better come in,' she murmured, blushing and fiddling with the floppy bow.

'I came to take Shipley for a run...'

In the doorway of the living room, Chesterton Wendlebury

beamed. 'My dear lady. Have you come to help Marina prepare for her book club?' His voice boomed.

Libby shook her head. 'Dog walking.'

'Ah. Do you have the redoubtable Bear with you?'

'He's at home with Max.' Finding the man here was a surprise, but Libby wasn't going to waste the opportunity. 'Mr Wendlebury.' She took a slow breath. 'I believe you might have known my husband.'

'Oh? What makes you think that?' His voice purred.

'Trevor – that's my husband – brought us all here for a holiday a few years ago. He had business in the area and spent almost every day driving off to meetings with clients.'

Wendlebury inclined his head in a vague non-committal gesture.

Libby ploughed on. 'After that holiday, my husband changed. I know that, around that time, he became involved in shady business deals.'

'Ah.' Wendlebury crossed one leg over the other. 'I recognise the influence of Mr Ramshore on your information. I've often wondered about him. A banker, taking early retirement, making frequent trips abroad.'

He smiled, showing large, tombstone teeth. *Like a shark.* 'Oh, yes, Mrs Forest, I've made it my business to check up on him; a financial wizard with a burning desire to interfere where he has no business.'

He broke off as Marina arrived with a tray of coffee. 'Marina, Mrs Forest and I were talking over old times. I expect, like most people in town, you thought she was new to the area?'

Marina gave an easy laugh. 'Plenty of summer visitors come back here to retire. Not that you've been taking it easy. You're always busy with something.' She adjusted the scarves at her neck, settling back onto her pale sofa.

'Did you know my husband, Marina?'

Marina glanced at Wendlebury, and away. 'We met once or twice. He came here a few times, without you and the children. On business, of course.'

Libby's next question was drowned by a crash that echoed through the house and brought Marina to her feet. 'Shipley,' she shouted. 'That dog. What mess has he made, now?'

Libby took Shipley off her hands as soon as she could and walked for over an hour on the beach, her head full of unanswered questions about Trevor's activities.

* * *

Next day, Libby leaned on Max's doorbell. *Come on. Wake up.* Her eyes were gritty from a night tossing and turning, puzzling over the connection between Wendlebury and Trevor. Flashes of memory from that first visit to Exham left her astonished she could have been so stupid. The children were still young then, and money tight, but Trevor hadn't wanted Libby to work.

'We need you at home to look after us,' he insisted, and Libby, wanting to be a good wife for the man she loved, took his words as signs of affection. She'd stayed at home, worrying about her husband. He spent hours alone in his study, and when he came out, he could be distracted and off-hand.

Libby decided he was working too hard and suggested a holiday. 'The English seaside. Buckets and spades for the kids, fish and chips for dinner.'

Trevor grinned and the lines of worry faded. 'One of my clients, Pritchards, has a head office on Exmoor. We could stay at the seaside in Exham on Sea. Let's combine business and pleasure for a week.' That was how they came to visit Exham. It was all her fault. How could she have forgotten?

Maybe she'd deliberately wiped it from her memory, because after that week, Trevor grew more distant, angry and unkind, and more critical of his wife. He spent long hours in the office or on business trips, his hair turned grey and he drank heavily, but Libby never dared speak of it. She watched, helpless, from the side-lines as her loving husband gradually disappeared, to be replaced by a cold, angry stranger.

If only she'd stood up to Trevor, tried to find out what was going on, maybe she could have made a difference. She shuddered. What if she'd discovered his criminal dealings? What could a wife do – shop him to the police? Or, could she have put a stop to it all? She'd never know, but one thing was certain. She'd let no one make a fool of her again. That's why she was here, on Max's doorstep, at a crazy early hour; to discover the truth about him.

The door opened. 'Whatever time do you think this is?' Max's hair stood in spikes on top of his head. In dressing gown and bare feet, rubbing fingers over early-morning beard stubble, he squinted at Libby. 'This had better be an emergency.'

She pushed past. 'I want an explanation from you, Max Ramshore.'

'Can I make coffee, first?'

'Answers first, then coffee.'

'That serious?' He led the way to the study, his private sanctum. Part of Libby registered the gesture. Maybe she'd get some honesty, for once.

She pushed a pile of documents at him and waited, foot tapping, taut with anxiety, as he fumbled in his desk for reading glasses before scanning the first page.

'We've already talked about these.' He sounded perfectly reasonable. 'We know your husband had a portfolio of houses, bought with money from criminal activities.' He shot a glance at

Libby. 'Trevor was just the admin man.' Libby waved a hand, impatient. This was old news.

She grabbed the pile of papers so agitated, she could hardly get her tongue round the words. 'What if Trevor's death wasn't an accident? He had a sudden heart attack. Not uncommon, I know, in a middle-aged man who drank and smoked and took no exercise, so how hard did the pathologist look for another cause of death? How did Trevor really die?'

Max leaned forward and took Libby's hands. 'You said it yourself. Your husband was a middle-aged man under a huge amount of stress. Why would you imagine he died from anything but a heart attack?'

Libby snatched her hands away and stared at Max, wondering what she was really seeing. Her voice was hard. 'Trevor had links to Exham on Sea. We came here when the children were young, and around that time, Trevor changed. He became a different person. He'd been kind and loving when we first married.' Tears slid down her cheeks. 'I know he loved me, once. Over the years, he became more controlling; telling me I was stupid, stopping me from seeing friends. It was gradual, and I didn't realise it was happening until he'd turned me into some sort of door mat. But I can see, now, that person wasn't the real Trevor. Maybe he was just weak. He got into bad company, couldn't find the way out of the mess he was in, and the result was terrible stress.' She could barely speak, for tears. 'If only he'd told me the truth, we could have sorted it all out.'

'Even if it meant prison?'

Libby wiped the tears away with the back of her hand. 'Even then. He should have trusted me. I could have helped, somehow.' Max walked to the window and back. Libby let the silence grow, but as each second ticked past, the knot in her chest tightened until every breath hurt and she couldn't stand it any longer. She whispered. 'Did – did you know about Trevor? Tell me, Max. Stop pretending.' When he turned, his face told the truth. 'You did. You knew what my husband was up to. You knew about the money and the properties from the start.'

Her fingers shook. Trevor's paper slid from her grasp scattering on the floor. 'You knew who I was, before I even arrived in Exham.' Every moment with Max flashed through Libby's mind. That first meeting, when he'd walked past her house, taking Bear for exercise. Why had he chosen to go that way when he could be on the beach or in the fields? Later that same day, he'd come into the bakery as if by accident and whisked Libby away for coffee. She shook her head, trying to clear it, letting in the stark truth. 'You've been watching me ever since I arrived in Exham.'

He put a hand on her arm, but she shook it off, spitting out bitter words. 'I understand, Max. I can see it all, now. You thought I was one of Trevor's – what should I call it – accomplices? You got close to me, deliberately, so I'd lead you to my husband's ill-gotten gains. And all the time I thought – I hoped...' She clenched her jaw, refusing to cry. 'Just tell me one thing, Max. How did Trevor die? Did you, or one of your shady friends, kill him?'

There. She'd said it. The shocking words were out. Her head was spinning, her heart thudding, blood hammering in her ears. She feared she was about to faint. Max gripped her arm, fingers digging in to her flesh. His eyes, usually so blue, glowed dark in a white face. 'Is that what you think? Do you honestly believe I'm a killer?'

Libby gulped. 'I – I don't want you to be.' She forced the words through dry lips.

Max let his hands drop. 'I had nothing to do with Trevor's death, although I can't blame you if you don't believe me.' With gentle fingers, he took one of Libby's hands. 'I'll tell you the truth. You're right about some of it. I did know who you were when you moved to Exham. I thought you'd come to tidy up Trevor's loose ends and my job was to stop you. I was looking for the mastermind behind the whole criminal conspiracy, and I needed to get close to you, so you could lead me there.'

Libby pulled her hand away. Her throat burned. 'You followed me.'

'You didn't notice a thing until I made the mistake of walking Bear too close to your house one morning and he got into a scrap with Fuzzy.'

'Which Fuzzy won.'

'She did. That cat's as feisty as her owner. Believe me, Libby, I soon realised you had nothing to do with your husband's crimes.'

'Am I supposed to be grateful?' Her fingers itched to slap his face. It would serve him right. 'Anyway, what made you decide I was innocent?'

'You were happy to get involved in police business. If you'd been a real criminal, you'd have let the authorities deal with the body under the lighthouse. I could see you were one of two things. Either you were a criminal and hopelessly incompetent, or you were innocent and nosy.'

She let that pass. 'So that's why you were keen to work with me. To see if I was what I seemed to be.'

He nodded. 'When I realised the truth, I was – well...' He fell silent. 'I'm sorry.'

'Sorry? Is that supposed to make it all right? You lied to me. And all the time I thought...' She shook her head, trying to clear it, struggling to think. What would she have done in Max's shoes? She didn't have to think for long before recognising the answer. She'd investigate, of course, as he'd done.

Max had known she was innocent since last autumn's murder at the lighthouse. She'd been no more use to him in his hunt for the person at the top of the criminal tree, but nevertheless, he'd stayed by her side, ready to help, watching out for her. She whispered, 'In Bristol, I asked if we had a relationship...'

Max slid one arm round her shoulders and pulled her close. 'I was cruel. You took me by surprise. I'd taken so much care to keep my distance, trying to pretend I wasn't falling for you. I never imagined you gave a fig for me. I thought it was all one way. In Bristol, I panicked and had a few second thoughts. What if I'd got it wrong and you were Trevor's accomplice, after all? Maybe, because I wanted you to be innocent, I was making a big mistake.' He grimaced. 'I'm not much good at relationships. Never have been. I couldn't believe my luck, that I stood a chance of getting this one right. So, I blew it all.'

'You should have trusted me.'

'I know. I was a fool. But I want to put it on the record, now. I've cared about you the whole time, Libby Forest, from the moment you first shouted abuse at me in the street. I'd love you, even if you were a master criminal.'

20

FRENCH TOAST

'Well, that was worth waiting for.' Max's kiss lasted a long time, until Bear, whose humans had spent far too long ignoring him, finished all the food in his dish, gobbled a few titbits left on the table, and came looking for action. He arrived on the sofa, all over-sized paws and wet nose, forcing Max and Libby apart. Which was just as well, Libby decided, as she had a hundred questions to ask.

Max grabbed the dog by his collar and led him away. 'He lives in the back place. Used to be a gun room, I suppose, when the squire lived here, but Bear's learned to open the door. I'm going to have to change the lock.'

As Max filled the dog's water bowl, Libby made tea and French toast and laid down a few ground rules. 'I'm not standing for any more secrets. I lived half my married life in the dark. If we're going to – you know.' She knew she was blushing. 'If we're going to be together, I need to trust you. You have to tell me everything you know about Trevor.'

'Fair enough, I suppose. Trouble is, I've got used to being secretive. It's a habit, these days. Let me try to put it all in order.'

He chewed in silence for a moment. 'I'll start at the beginning. I was called in as part of an investigation into Trevor's insurance company because there seemed to be some creative accounting going on. I'm afraid Trevor wasn't a very efficient fraudster.' Libby winced, bracing herself for the worst. 'HMRC picked it up first and passed it on. My job then was to re-audit the finances.'

Libby nodded. 'The tax people never miss a trick, do they?'

'We could see Trevor was a weak link. He came down to Exham several times, after that first visit with you and the family, and that made us curious. I wasn't living here at that time. You and I didn't meet.' He stopped talking, his eyes on Libby. She knew what he was thinking because Libby was wondering as well. What would have happened if the two of them had met, back then?

He looked away and the spell broke. 'He had plenty of insurance customers here but all the paperwork seemed above board. I realised someone around here was running things. That's when I moved back. I had the perfect cover because I grew up in Exham. Local people trust me and I was the best one to untangle the relationships in the area. Families are so closely woven. Everyone is somebody's aunt, or step-brother, or second cousin twice removed, and they all look out for each other.'

'It's rather lovely, in a way,' Libby put in. 'Families are sometimes all you have.' She thought of Ali, on the other side of the world, sending lengthy emails each week, and Robert, planning to bring his girlfriend home. She was almost sure he'd be announcing their engagement.

She bit into her toast. Max looked so serious, his brows almost meeting. Libby had to pick up her coffee cup to keep from stroking his hair. 'I found a reference to property in Leeds and we sent one of our men up there to rent it, under cover.'

'Your friend Cal James and his wife. The ones living in Trevor's house.'

'Yes. Well, the wife was Cal's idea – part of the cover story. What is it?' He frowned. 'What's so funny?'

'Cover stories, laundering money, Mr Big in the Exham area. Who would have thought it in a quiet seaside town like this? It's hard to believe.'

Max's lips curved but the smile didn't reach his eyes. 'Unfortunately, it's true. We're very close to catching the person at the top of the tree but I don't want you any further involved.'

'Why not? You can't be afraid anyone's going to shoot me, are you?'

This time, Max didn't even try to smile. 'That's exactly what I'm afraid of. You're too good an investigator. That'll be fine when we're operating as Ramshore and Forest, Investigators at Large, but it might put you in danger with Trevor's masters.'

'Forest and Ramshore, you mean.'

The smile reappeared. 'Whatever. I want you to be safe, Libby. We're close to finishing this business but don't forget, the criminals have been watching you, as I was. Will you promise to be careful and stop poking your nose in everywhere when I'm not around?'

Libby sighed. 'I suppose I'd better come clean.' She told Max about the visit to Marina's house. 'Chesterton Wendlebury was there. I think they're having some sort of a liaison. In her own home.' She stopped, thinking about Marina's husband, Henry. Did he really have no idea what was going on? 'I'm convinced Chesterton Wendlebury's behind it all, though I don't have any evidence.'

'You really don't like that man, do you?'

She shivered. 'His eyes are too close together.' Max was silent.

Libby narrowed her eyes. 'What aren't you telling me? I thought we were being honest with each other.'

His sigh was heavy. 'It's not so much Wendlebury, as his company.'

'Pritchards.' Libby was triumphant. 'I knew it.'

'Most of their business is above board. Cut-throat, of course, but that's how they make money.'

'They tried to buy out the bakery for pennies when it had to shut.'

'As I said, that's business, but they were also running local gangs of petty criminals; the vehicle ringers and cannabis growers. The police closed most down but they let a few continue so they could gather more evidence. Joe's been part of the team working on that; he's known what I've been doing all along.'

'And that's why you two kept up the pretence of not speaking.'

'Some of that was genuine. I was a pretty bad father. But we rub along most of the time.'

Libby drained the last drops from her mug. 'I'm still puzzled by Trevor taking out mortgages on his houses. Seems odd to me.

'It's all part of the scam, laundering money and covering his tracks.'

'How exactly did it work?'

'His criminal contacts put money into his bank accounts – he had several you never knew about, and he bought the houses using a mix of that tainted cash and short-term bank mortgages. He thought his bosses wouldn't check on him – they have dozens of properties all over the country. He foolishly gambled on them taking their eyes off him.

'The gang handed the tenants of Trevor's properties enough cash to cover the rent. That way, more dirty money changed hands and became legitimate. But Trevor thought he could hold on to the properties for five years, until the mortgage terms expired, then sell them under his own name and keep the proceeds.

At the same time, he used his job as an insurance agent to organise inflated payments for repairs that were then carried out at a fraction of the price, while he kept the difference. Unfortunately for Trevor, he didn't understand how ruthless his contacts could be – or that they were checking up on him all the time.'

'He was trying to double-cross the bosses but they found out?'

'His insurance activities put them at risk. Once they suspected he was syphoning money off for himself, they looked more closely and saw the danger. If the authorities followed the same trail, the entire money laundering empire could unravel, so they got rid of the weak link. Unfortunately, the weak link was Trevor.'

Libby drew a long breath. 'So, they had him killed.'

21

LEMON CAKE

Beryl, a long-term member of the Exham History Society, sat in a corner of Marina's room dressed in her favourite shade of brown, sipping Earl Grey tea. Her cup rattled in its saucer, her fingers trembling with excitement. She was about to present her paper to the group.

The First Post Office in Exham had been opened by Beryl's great grandfather, and she'd been waiting a long time for the opportunity to tell the tale.

She had high hopes of today's meeting. True, it had been convened to celebrate the end of the great Glastonbury Tor murder mystery and the part in the story played by the historic amber beads. Jemima Bakewell, currently eating biscuits and chatting with a couple of society members, was giving the main talk, but surely there would be a few moments at the end to fill?

'I wouldn't get your hopes up,' Libby whispered, as Detective Sergeant Joe Ramshore and his father, Max, arrived together, looking awkward and uncomfortable as they perched on two of Marina's antique chairs.

'Have more cake, darling.' Marina offered Beryl a slice of

Libby's acclaimed whisky and lemon cake. 'It'll settle your nerves.'

All the society regulars had come for this special meeting. Even Samantha Watson found time in her important schedule to attend. She held one of Marina's bone china cups in her left hand, little finger raised, over-sized engagement ring on prominent display. She was due to marry Chief Inspector Arnold in three months.

George Edwards gave his wife's apologies. She'd sprained her ankle. Libby suspected George's wife's ailments were an excuse; after every meeting, he took home a large doggy bag of cake.

Chesterton Wendlebury arrived with a flourish, heaved his bulk into the largest, most comfortable armchair, and beamed round the room. 'So kind of you to invite me. I'm agog to hear more of Mrs Forest's adventures.'

'Well, if we're all here,' began Angela Miles, one of the society's founder members, 'I'll ask Libby to tell us about the latest events on Glastonbury Tor.'

The society listened, enthralled, as Libby told the sad story of Catriona's murder, so far in the past. 'It was hard to get at the truth, after so long. People remember the same event in different ways, even in the best of circumstances. In this case, our university students from the sixties were ashamed of things they'd done or said. Each of them tried to distance themselves from the truth. They couldn't even agree on the character of Catriona, their friend. Was she beautiful and kind, or greedy and selfish? Why did she hand her child over to adoptive parents; for the sake of appearances, or her career, or to keep the professor's love? We'll never know, for sure, but her death led directly to the death of John Williams so many years later.'

No one interrupted, even as she took a gulp of tea. 'Professor Perivale was confident he'd escaped punishment for pushing

Catriona out of the window. I don't believe he was capable of love. He was driven by a desperate need to maintain his reputation.

'Imagine how such an arrogant, self-absorbed man felt when he heard about a retrospective exhibition of his old colleague's work. Those photographs could stir up memories of Catriona's death and put the professor's reputation at risk. He couldn't allow that. He'd managed to commit the perfect crime once, so he was confident he could do it again. Without a second thought, he killed John Williams.'

Joe took up the story. 'The professor blackmailed a failing student into giving him an alibi for the time of the murder and setting off an explosion in his own house. As he hoped, that threw everyone off the scent. He used a fertiliser based explosive, following instructions from the internet. We found them in his browsing history.'

Max grinned. 'He underestimated the force of the blast and landed up in hospital. He wasn't as clever as he thought but he did succeed in throwing us off the scent for a while.'

Joe finished the tale. 'We interviewed the professor's student, who soon realised a failing grade was preferable to a conviction as an accessory to murder. He admitted there had been no tutorial that morning and the professor's alibi for the time of John Williams' murder fell apart. He's safely in custody now, condescending to the police officers and convinced he's still cleverer than the rest of us.'

As the story ended, Marina poured more tea. 'Today, we're also welcoming Miss Jemima Bakewell to our society. She'd going to tell us a little of the prehistory of the area. Let's give her a warm welcome.'

The society clapped politely and Jemima launched into her lecture on the Iron Age. She'd borrowed Katy's necklace from Catriona's son, Sam, for the occasion, and the society members were enthralled by the chance to see and touch a 2,000 year old artefact.

'Luckily for us,' Jemima finished, 'the necklace contains no precious metal, so Sam and Katy can keep it safe. We've registered it with the Portable Antiquities Scheme and Katy can pass it on to the Museum of Somerset, in Taunton, when she's older. In the meantime, they have one bead already on display – the one Libby found at Deer Leap.'

She took off her spectacles and polished them vigorously. She'd already confessed her part in the Deer Leap escapade to Libby. 'I wanted to protect Malcolm, so I tried to add another myth to the mix. Silly, I know – I was panicking.'

As Jemima finished, Beryl reached into her handbag, groping for her own speech, but Libby held up a hand. 'Sorry, Beryl, there's something important I have to say.'

Out of Libby's line of sight, someone coughed. Marina offered cake. 'Another story, darling? Do be quick, the cake's almost finished.'

'This one's personal. When my husband brought me to Exham, many years ago, I had no idea he was setting up contacts with local criminals. For years, local vehicle ringing and cannabis businesses filtered money through Trevor. Max spent months tracking financial deals and all the trails led back here, to Exham.'

She looked from one face to another, searching for signs of guilt. 'One company in particular make money buying up properties cheaply.'

Someone murmured, 'Pritchards.'

'Exactly. We've all heard they stop at nothing to ruin small businesses. Max had a look at their affairs.'

Marina rubbed her hands together. 'Ooh, Libby, this is too exciting.'

Samantha Watson set her cup in its saucer. 'I'm quite sure the police are far better placed to uncover this – what shall I call it – nest of thieves, than an amateur sleuth like you. I suggest you leave everything to them and stop poking your nose in where it isn't wanted.'

Joe intervened. 'Detective Chief Inspector Arnold is well aware of the situation, I can assure you, Mrs Watson. I have his full authority.'

Samantha tossed her head. 'Then, I suggest you do your job and catch the criminal.'

'That's exactly what I'm here to do.' Someone gasped. 'But I'd like Mrs Forest to finish the story.'

Libby cleared her throat. 'I wondered who Trevor knew in Exham, and two people were at the top of the list.' She turned to Chesterton Wendlebury. 'You admitted to being on the board of Pritchards, and I've bumped into you in some strange places over the past year; at the county show, riding with Marina on the Levels.'

Wendlebury smiled, the shark teeth prominent. 'My dear lady, if your friend Max has investigated my business affairs, you must know they're completely in order.'

Max was smiling. 'I've read every budget and report you've had your hands on, Wendlebury. You've done a great job. I couldn't locate a single suspicious account or strange payment. No, it isn't you at the top of the tree. You provide cover for someone far cleverer.'

Libby said, 'I'm afraid it's someone who's always been at the centre of things in Exham. Someone who knows everyone in town and lives a wealthy, innocent life. Someone who made friends with me as soon as I arrived in the town, knew all about my husband's business affairs, and wanted to keep a very close eye on me.'

She examined each face. Only one pair of eyes looked away.

'In fact, the genius at the top of the whole pyramid of crime is our generous host and town busybody, Marina Stallworthy, aided and abetted by her quiet, hen-pecked husband, Henry.'

* * *

The shock of Marina Stallworthy's arrest reverberated through Exham for weeks. The community lost interest in the murder on the Tor, as the townspeople realised they'd never quite trusted Marina, and always suspected there was something odd about the inoffensive Henry.

'Marina made sure I knew all about her fictitious affair with Chesterton Wendlebury,' Libby admitted, lying on Max's sofa, Bear at her feet. 'She knew I'd tell you about it. Like everyone else, I hardly gave Henry a thought.'

'They made the perfect criminal couple,' Max agreed. 'Marina at the centre of the community, watching and manipulating, while Henry, almost unnoticed, directed operations through his old client, Wendlebury. I don't believe Wendlebury ever understood what was going on. Underneath the country gentleman act, there's precious little intelligence. Marina was at the centre of a complicated web. It will be a long time before they come to trial.'

'Will you be involved?'

'I'll be giving evidence, with the greatest of pleasure.'

A shiver travelled up Libby's spine. 'We still don't know whether Trevor's death was an accident, or murder. He was cremated, so we'll probably never be sure unless Marina or Henry decides to tell us. I'm afraid they're not likely to do that.'

Max drew her head on to his shoulder. 'Can you live with that? Not knowing for sure?'

'I shall have to. At least, there are good things to look forward to. My son emailed me this week and he's coming home, bringing his girlfriend. I'm almost sure there's a wedding on the horizon and I'll be busy making the biggest, grandest cake Exham's ever seen.'

Max fetched a bottle of champagne and popped it open. Libby said, 'We ought to drink a toast: to cake, chocolates and our partnership, Ramshore and Forest, Private Investigators.'

Max's raised glass sparkled with condensation. 'I'll drink to that, with just one proviso. Let's toast our real future. Here's to you and me: Libby and Max.'

ACKNOWLEDGMENTS

A big thank you to everyone who helped in the production of this book, including friends and work colleagues who encouraged me to write, my family who read and check every word and my husband for his unfailing support.

I'd especially like to thank my new publishers, Boldwood Books, for their confidence in me, and especially Caroline Ridding, my editor, Rose Fox, for copy edits and proofing and Nick Castle for some great cover art.

I'd like to reassure all my neighbours and the people of Burnham on Sea that the characters in my stories are completely fictional – especially the criminals.

Finally, thank you to the real Bear, a gentle giant of a dog who lived next door to us for a few years in Belgium. Without knowing it, he became the inspiration for the Exham on Sea sheepdog, Bear.

MORE FROM FRANCES EVESHAM

We hope you enjoyed reading *Murder on the Tor*. If you did, please leave a review.

If you'd like to gift a copy, this book is also available as an ebook, digital audio download and audiobook CD.

Sign up to become a Frances Evesham VIP and receive a free copy of the Exham-on-Sea Kitchen Cheat Sheet. You will also receive news, competitions and updates on future books:

https://bit.ly/FrancesEveshamSignUp

ALSO BY FRANCES EVESHAM

The Exham-On-Sea Murder Mysteries

Murder at the Lighthouse

Murder on the Levels

Murder on the Tor

Murder at the Cathedral

Murder at the Bridge

Murder at the Castle

Murder at the Gorge

The Ham-Hill Murder Mysteries

A Village Murder

ABOUT THE AUTHOR

Frances Evesham is the author of the hugely successful Exham-on-Sea Murder Mysteries set in her home county of Somerset. In her spare time, she collects poison recipes and other ways of dispatching her unfortunate victims. She likes to cook with a glass of wine in one hand and a bunch of chillies in the other, her head full of murder—fictional only.

Visit Frances' website: https://franceseevesham.com/

Follow Frances on social media:

twitter.com/francesevesham

facebook.com/frances.evesham.writer

bookbub.com/authors/frances-evesham

instagram.com/francesevesham

ABOUT BOLDWOOD BOOKS

Boldwood Books is a fiction publishing company seeking out the best stories from around the world.

Find out more at www.boldwoodbooks.com

Sign up to the Book and Tonic newsletter for news, offers and competitions from Boldwood Books!

http://www.bit.ly/bookandtonic

We'd love to hear from you, follow us on social media:

facebook.com/BookandTonic
twitter.com/BoldwoodBooks
instagram.com/BookandTonic

CPSIA information can be obtained
at www.ICGtesting.com
Printed in the USA
LVHW082147170822
726253LV00032B/1146